Dovetail Joint

and other stories

Dovetail Joint

and other stories

Lenore Rowntree

To Vivian + John,
Love you both.
Lenore

This is a work of fiction. Characters and incidents are either the product of the author's imagination or used fictionally. Any resemblance to actual persons, living or dead, is entirely coincidental.

Library and Archives Canada Cataloguing in Publication

Rowntree, Lenore Ruth, author
Dovetail Joint and other stories / Lenore Rowntree.

Short stories.
ISBN 978-0-9939223-0-5 (paperback)

I. Title.

PS8635.O887D68 2015 C813'.6 C2015-903519-8

Published by Quadra Books
Victoria, BC, Canada
www.quadrabooks.com

For Jeff,
who is all of and none
of the men in these stories

A Collection of Linked Stories

Dovetail Joint

Vanessa eyes the knot at the end of the plank laid out on her workbench. She moves a hand plane along the grain, careful not to bruise the wood with her bracelet. A curl shaves back toward her face, throwing up a pinch of scent. It makes her want to put her tongue on the streak of exposed pine, lodge a molecule of bitter pitch in the back of her throat.

The instructor at the front of the class makes the almost imperceptible dip of his head that signals he's about to talk. He's a compact man named Luke whose hair is the same colour as the sawdust that comes up from around the knot Vanessa is planing—brown with hints of gold. Her body straightens to listen as she watches a red glow emerge from beneath his shirt, move up his throat and into his cheeks.

"Everybody come and have a look at what Heather has done with her corners," he says.

Vanessa sets the plane down, ready to move, but she waits. She does not want to be first up beside Luke again. While she's paused, she wipes at the beard of shavings that hang from the front of her mohair sweater. A dumb choice for woodworking class, even if cerise does make her look younger. She knows from years in fashion merchandising this is one of the best colours for a cool-toned brunette like herself. *Try to look at the pulse*, she used to tell her clerks, *if the veins are blue the customer is cool.*

As she starts to make her move, she gets hung up waiting behind Ernesto, who works at the bench next to hers and has taken this moment to sip espresso from his thermos. He's got his foot up on his stool and his body turned in the aisle so there's no easy way to get past him as he slowly drinks. By the time she is finally able to glide forward, she's so far back from the action she can't see anything. She can only hear that Luke is talking.

"These brass guards Heather has put on her box are practical for a really functional piece. She's done a fine job. Everybody take a look and think about how you're going to finish your own corners. And don't forget about the dovetail joint for those of you who can handle it."

She can see Luke hold something up in the air, but she isn't sure what it is and doesn't dare venture forward to have a closer look. As she walks back to her station, she silently mocks the *Heather-this-Heather-that* of it all. It's only the second week and already she's sick of so much about Heather. Why are the blondes always the centre of attention? Especially when Ernesto is clearly the most accomplished—though she can't blame Luke for not wanting to move in too close on that one—wine and salami breath with overtones of coffee. This much she can tell just by looking at him and his swarthy near-neck beard.

Vanessa's head is down close to the plank when she feels the heat of a body behind her. She thinks it might be Ernesto, so she doesn't look up and is startled when she hears Luke's voice over her shoulder.

"Move the plane with more assurance."

He puts his hand on top of hers and together they glide along the plank in one smooth motion.

"That's better," he says.

Luke smells of pine. When she sneaks a sidelong glance she sees that what she'd thought was a streak of grey is only specks of sawdust sprinkled in his hair. His hand looks surprisingly youthful on top of hers, their fingers lightly interlaced, his tanned and hers almost translucent white. At the proximity of his youth, her hand makes an almost imperceptible movement of discontent underneath his. They both feel it.

"Easy," he says.

She smiles shyly and, unsure she can continue, takes her hand off the plane. When their eyes lock for just a second, the strain is intense, as if the muscles behind her eyeballs might spasm. She looks down from his face and sees a faded insignia on his t-shirt: Hart House, University of Toronto. She keeps her eyes averted, gazes at his shoes while she digests this new information—he's university educated, his eyes look wise.

She starts to convince herself again that despite his boyish skin, he could be close to forty.

WHEN VANESSA'S HUSBAND turned sixty, he'd taken the package the board offered for his twenty-five years in the trenches as a high school principal. Vanessa said then she didn't want him to feel alone in this step, so she'd leave her work too. But the truth is the colour and light in her job had dimmed the day she was told her *demographic* (read *age*) made her perfect for the newly created position of executive buyer. What this really meant is that she was no longer going to be lead buyer for an exclusive retail chain, rather she was to take direction from a woman who was nearly twenty years her junior and whose sensibility tended toward grunge.

Vanessa knows now that she made the decision to retire too hastily. Dick has adjusted slightly better, although he still spends too much of his time walking Lucy, their aged and adored King Charles spaniel. But now she has definitely gone house-crazy. She misses travelling the world searching for fashions, haggling with exotic dealers and brokers, and she overfills her days with largely irrelevant community meetings and uninspiring courses.

For some reason, the description of the woodworking course had been different. It had leapt from the calendar of options advertised in the newspaper—*build your own toolbox in just 8 weeks.* When she'd read the ad, she'd thought she could use the box to store the Japanese carving tools Dick had given her the year before for her fiftieth birthday. The tools were something she'd said in passing that she wanted, and he'd taken her seriously. At her birthday dinner, he'd said to her, "Nothing's too fine for you." What he hadn't said was that he'd been observing her unhappy spiral, and he'd grasped at the only thing that seemed to hold her amusement for more than a few seconds.

Most importantly, Vanessa knew she needed to build a box as proof she was actually doing something with her time. But she'd made a mistake when she registered for the workshop. She shouldn't have taken the discount offered for early seniors. In joining the 50+ group, she'd been making an honest effort to embrace the next stage, to stop shrinking back whenever Dick enveloped her in a bear hug of enthusiasm for their new life. Still, she'd been dismayed when she'd arrived at the first class to see the big red star beside her and Ernesto's names. Evidently, they were the only two who had taken the seniors' discount.

Afterward, she'd nearly dropped out. It had taken two hours each way to do the bus-subway-bus shuffle from their house in Leaside to the workshop in Swansea. She'd come home at the end of it with a nose full of pine dust, an attitude as wet and tired as the mid-October day it was, and a hate-on for Toronto Transit.

Although when she stopped to think about it, she realized she'd just had too much time sitting on a bus mulling over the misstep she'd made in giving away her age by virtue of her registration. But then there'd been that difficult conversation with Dick.

"Why don't you find a closer workshop?" he'd asked.

"There isn't another one like it," she'd said.

"What's this class again?"

"It's not the class, it's the instructor."

"Well, what's so special about the instructor?"

When she'd signed up, she'd imagined someone more like Ernesto would be teaching. Somebody stout, old-world, a man perhaps who'd spent too many years in the backyard tending grapes and staking tomato plants to have any sex appeal left. Instead it's the surprisingly arousing Luke, and she hadn't known how to answer Dick's question. So she'd been grateful when he'd left it hanging to bend over and give Lucy an affectionate pat.

"Okay, Lucy and I will drive you. We'll walk High Park while we wait for you. Won't we old girl?"

Lucy had given her head a shake and her collar had rattled. She, at least, liked the attention.

WHEN LUKE PAUSES at Vanessa's workbench, she stiffens. She hates that she can't feel relaxed around him.

"That's enough planing," he says. "Take a piece of medium sandpaper and see if you can straighten out that dimple. Look for the spirit in the wood."

"I'm trying," she mumbles.

It's week four already and she's barely ready to glue. Her hands still feel like two clubs when she works. The week before, Ernesto, already on to his second box, had stopped by to tell her, "Pretty lady, you try too hard. The wood has direction. All you have to do is help it." She wonders if perhaps too much advice is clouding her mind.

Luke moves on and stops at Ernesto's bench, where the two of them huddle over a sketch.

"What's this box going to be for?" Luke asks.

"Going to give it to my granddaughter," Ernesto answers.

"Is she a woodworker?"

"Oh no, my friend. She is seven years old. It can be for her trousseau."

Ernesto sticks his barrel chest out. Vanessa can't stand it—*as if any kid these days has a trousseau.* There's a sheen on his forehead that tells her he smells of garlic today. She watches Luke dip his head, "Everybody over here. I want you to see how Ernesto has mitred his corners."

Vanessa sets down the sandpaper—at least they're not being summoned to the altar of Heather this time—she positions herself at the back of the group leaning on the workbench behind her. She's in a comfortable space where she can watch Luke without him seeing her. But she isn't aware how intensely she's absorbed the rhythms of his body, hers swaying gently when he bends to hug the wood as he talks, until she hears him say, "Then you can insert a cloth liner to make the box more of a showpiece than something functional." Instantly, she is angry with herself. She's been busy watching without listening again, she's missed the explanation of something she might like to do with her own box.

Too frustrated to begin listening now, she lets her mind wander completely. She is thinking how well Luke wears his work jeans when suddenly her thoughts leap to Dick and aged Lucy. In her mind's eye, she can see the two of them slowly moving down the curve of Park Drive toward Grenadier Pond, a place where Lucy loves to pretend she's a retriever on the hunt. But this time of year the road can be covered in a slick of ice, and the wind can move across Lake Ontario with a ferocity that makes even Lucy hunch into her doggie coat—though Vanessa imagines the few strands of brown hair that Dick has left, the ones he insists on greasing and combing back, would still be sticking down. She's watching Dick give Lucy's leash a gentle tug, when she hears Luke ask, "What are you going to line it with?"

"Pink velvet," Ernesto says.

Oh my god, what is Ernesto thinking? Vanessa can't help but roll her eyes. When her eyeballs descend from the nether region of her head, she realizes the class is staring at her. Had she make a sound too? Emitted some exasperated sigh?

"Did you have a question, Vanessa?" Luke asks.

"No. No thanks," she answers.

BY THE SIXTH WEEK, Lucy has figured out what it means when Vanessa carries the duffel bag of tools to the garage, and they all get into the car to drive off. Lucy is so energized by the adventure, she leaps like a young puppy into the open passenger door to nestle at Vanessa's feet. The three of them are in front of the warehouse where the workshop is held when Lucy, excited to get started with the visit to the pond, burns out of the car the minute Vanessa opens the door. Lucy is running down the middle of the street, her paws sliding out from under her on the icy road, when Dick jumps sideways to save her from the garbage truck that barrels toward them. Vanessa holds her breath and waits for one of Lucy, Dick, or the truck to stop.

After the truck rumbles by, and Dick is standing safely at the side of the road with Lucy in his arms, Vanessa needs to spend a few moments sitting in the car to settle herself.

Her heart is still racing when she walks into the workshop and notices things are a little different. People are not bent over their benches, instead the man named Joe who works one down from Ernesto is talking. "I live near Kensington Market. Ernesto and I have been best friends since high school, when he first came here from Italy. He barely spoke a word of English then, but we worked together at the same table saw, so we learned to communicate through wood."

As Joe finishes, Ernesto hoists his espresso cup and says, "*Salute*, my friend."

Luke swings his eyes around toward Vanessa and says, "Hi there. Heather suggested, since we don't know much about one another, we should say a little about whatever we like. So what about you?"

Vanessa's immediate thought is, *Have I missed Luke's intro?* Her hands shake, but she wills herself to be calm and says, "This is my first woodworking class and I'm really enjoying it."

Luke stares at her for a moment until it registers that this is all she's going to say. When he moves on, she quietly sets out her glue and clamps, and barely listens to the others, until Luke begins to speak.

"My turn, I guess. Well, I live in Slabtown where I've been working alone for a lot of years restoring an old Victorian farmhouse. It's the place where I've honed my woodworking skills."

Heather puts her hand up, pink pearl nail polish flashing. "Where do you find the discipline to keep working like that on an old place?"

Luke smiles. "At the risk of butchering what I think some opera singer said, *It's not discipline, it's devotion.* Woodworking is a spiritual thing for me. Almost sacred."

Vanessa stares at her clamps and wonders if she has any discipline. She knows she's lacking in devotion. Possibly spirituality too. She's nervous when Luke starts to walk toward her.

"Big day. Putting it all together," he says.

Her hands tremble. She notices he is wearing his Hart House t-shirt again. To distract them both from her shaking hands, she asks, "Do you like Hart House?"

"Oh yeah. Do you know it? Such beautiful *cinquefoil* shapes in the trusses."

Vanessa says nothing. She doesn't know what *cinquefoil* means and has to admit she never noticed the trusses when she was a student at the university.

Luke turns and moves toward the front of the class where she thinks he's going to make a group comment, but instead he picks up an L-shaped piece of wood and carries it back to her.

"This is the dovetail joint I showed the class a couple of weeks back. I think you missed seeing it. Maybe next box, you can use this technique on your corners." He sets the shape down on her workbench, so she can see the interlocking pieces of wood at the corner. They look a lot like his tanned and her translucent fingers joined.

"You can keep the sample," he says. "Study it when the time comes for your next challenge."

Luke leaves his offering and for a moment she thinks she should return it for fear of what it might represent.

VANESSA IS IN THE KITCHEN feeding raw carrots and apples into the juicer. She likes to stare out the window and let her thoughts drift while she listens to the sound of the machine masticating. By the time she's adding the beets for Dick's blood pressure, she's pondering what Luke's major might have been at university. She settles on Philosophy, deciding this for no reason other than he seems to be a deeply solitary and contemplative person. She's having fun with the carpentry of his character, assembling a truly heroic figure, when Dick walks into the kitchen and disrupts her prince building.

"Looks like there's been a bloody murder in here," he says.

She steps back to see red beet juice flowing down the cupboards and onto the floor.

"Oh god, sorry. The jug shifted and most of your beet juice is on the floor."

"That's okay," Dick says, as he moves toward the cupboard to get the mop, "I'm not planning on having a stroke tonight."

After the mess is cleaned up, they're quiet over dinner, and when the dishes are loaded, Dick goes down to the basement to assemble his hunting gear. The next day, he and his buddies are set to go on an overnight to a wetland near Gananoque. It's a place they travel to every year, mostly to drink beer and swap stories, but occasionally to venture into a waterfowl blind and pretend to be duck hunters. Vanessa has never liked that they do this, but she knows, especially this year, it's good for Dick to get out. She says nothing and goes instead into the den to sit at the computer. She stares at the screen for a time before typing the word 'Slabtown' into Google search.

After some pecking, she finds a map that shows the town near the end of the Beaver Valley Road, just where the Beaver River heads away from the Blue Mountains before dumping into Georgian Bay. It looks to be about an hour and a half drive north of Toronto. It's an odd name, she thinks, curious she's never heard of it, but still it must be a decent size if it's a town.

She's about to turn off the computer when she sees a link to a property for sale on Slabtown Road. She decides to take a virtual tour, clicking through several photos until she comes to one that makes her stop. It's a shot taken on a sunny, summer day, and it shows a slab of concrete abutting the river where a mill must have been. The caption says *a favourite swimming hole.* In the picture there's a distant image of a man poised on the slab ready to dive into the river. The scene looks elegant and timeless.

Later in bed, she lies in the dark and listens to Dick breathe. He's not exactly snoring, it's more of a rhythmic pre-snore, but she knows when he starts out like this that once he's in full REM, the snore will be loud and continuous and she will not sleep. Before she lets herself get exasperated, she moves to the divan in the living room and nestles under the duvet she keeps there. She closes her eyes and the image of the man poised at the river is still there, only this time she is up close, and it is Luke. His hand holds hers, their fingers interlock, and the two of them are ready to dive into the river together. She thinks back, how his hand has already steadied hers when his body glided hers along the length of a plank. How but for an inch between them, he could have cupped her, completely enveloped her. She finds the fingers of one of her hands at the spot on her other hand where he had first touched her. Restless with the thought of him, and having no urge to curb desires she hasn't felt in a long time, she can hardly believe her body still works in the way that it does.

After her body is calm again, Lucy comes to lie on the floor beside her. Vanessa drops her hand to stroke the top of her head. "You're such a good doggie, Lucy," she says.

In the morning, Dick's voice startles her. "Go back to the bed, Vanessa. I'm sorry if I kept you awake. The guys are here. See you tomorrow. Come on girl."

Lucy picks herself up off the floor. Vanessa hears her paws click across the hardwood toward Dick and the open front door. She hears the sleeting rain outside, and burrows further into her duvet.

"Be careful," she croaks in a sleepy voice.

IN THE EARLY AFTERNOON, she decides to perk herself up by changing into some nice clothing. She puts her cerise sweater over a lacy camisole, pulls on new slim-leg black pants, and affixes a sterling locket around her neck. She adjusts the chain so the locket's silver heart reflects light up to her face. When she backs the car out of the garage between gusts of howling wind and sheets of black rain, she believes she's only going as far as Bayview Avenue to shop for groceries and treat herself to a cappuccino. But when the sun suddenly comes out, she finds herself following its light along Bayview to Highway 401, then across to the Islington exit where the ramp is infused with gold and beckons her to follow.

At the intersection of Finch, she stops at a donut shop for a coffee. She Googles Slabtown once more on her Blackberry. It seems farther now, but she's already on the edge of the city so why not keep going. She puts the Blackberry away, looks in the rearview mirror to refresh her lipstick and backs up the car.

By the time she arrives at Beaver Valley Road, the sky is no longer sunny and an icy wind is coming off Georgian Bay down the valley. As she nears the top of the road, close to the ski resorts, she starts to grip the wheel for fear of sliding. She's all the way to the t-intersection outside the town of Thornbury before she realizes she must have passed the turnoff to Slabtown.

On the way back, her wipers are moving so fast in the driving rain, she almost misses again the small, white sign pointing to Slabtown. She makes the turn onto the dippy cement road, which changes to a rutted, dirt lane as soon as it crosses the river. Slabtown, she realizes, is barely a hamlet.

The first house on her right is a lofted cathedral-style structure with a ghostly metal sculpture stalking the front yard. This is an artisan community, she thinks. She's busy focusing on a rammed-earth house in the middle of a small meadow to her left, when the car reminds her she's still driving by taking out a sign at the turn before the end of the road. She has to sit for a minute to think what to do. She doesn't want to get out because of the sheeting rain, but she knows she must, must try at least to right the sign.

She holds her pink umbrella with its sure-release titanium trigger over her head, while she stares at the flattened board that says Lucas Parker Cabinet Maker & Lumber Supplier. When she looks up, she sees that it is lying in the mud in front of an old Victorian house, and on the porch stands Luke Parker.

He starts across the yard holding a sweatshirt above his head.

"Hello, Vanessa," he calls.

She watches him pick his feet over the dips of wet grass and mud. Once he's near, he says, "I knew I'd have an unexpected visitor when I spotted a black fox in the field early this morning. Mind if I get under?"

Vanessa stares at him blankly. He gestures with his thumb toward her umbrella.

"Oh, sure. Sorry. Yes get under. And sorry I took out your sign, Lucas." She is embarrassed now, she's used his full name. She'd been reading the sign instead of looking at him.

When she'd set out, she'd had no intention of actually seeing him, but now that she's here and he is underneath her umbrella, close enough for a kiss if she'd been prepared, she has no clue what to do. Instead she asks, "What did you take at U of T?"

"What?"

"The Hart House t-shirt."

He looks at his chest to confirm he's not wearing the shirt.

"Okay. Yeah. That shirt. Where did I get it? I think they gave it to me after I finished restoring the bar in the old officer's dining hall."

"But what did you take at the university?"

"Never went to university myself."

Up close, even stripped of his university degree, cocooned under her pink umbrella, Vanessa confronts the bare truth of it. She is falling in love with this man.

"Luke," a woman's voice calls from the direction of the porch, "what are you doing out there?"

"Hey, honey. It's just one of my students. I'll be back in a sec."

"Cranberry scones are getting cold," the woman's voice continues.

"Stick 'em in the oven for a bit, hon."

"Okay."

Luke turns back to Vanessa. "Shauna, my wife," he says. "She teaches culinary arts." Then as if to prove she's good at it, he pats his stomach. "Best fed man in the county."

Vanessa wants to touch his belly too, yet as she thinks this, a wall of reason slams up through the ground and practically hits her with a physical force. He's married. He's happy. He's well-fed. His words in class—*I worked alone for many years*—merely meant *I worked alone.* They did not in any way mean *I am alone.*

She can't help herself, she turns to watch the backside of a curvaceous blonde and a tow-headed toddler disappear through the porch door. For a second, she's not sure she can continue standing. Her face and fingers are tingling with hurt and disappointment.

"Come on into the house and get dried off," Luke says. "Try a scone."

"Oh, no thanks, I can't. You're busy with family. But let me help you with your sign."

"Don't worry. I'll fix it tomorrow. Nobody's coming by today anyway. At least come on into the shop and take a look at that Rockwell lathe I've been telling the class about."

He starts walking back across the yard. Not really wanting to, but not knowing what else to do, Vanessa follows.

As they walk, Luke asks, "What are you doing out here anyway?"

"I was in Meaford and took a wrong turn." They both know this is nonsense, but he leaves it alone.

They move in on a post and beam shed that's been restored and added onto. Luke pushes on the door and an aromatic puff of warm air escapes from inside.

"That's hazelnut we're smelling. I'm working on a fancy ski cabin over at Devil's Glen. I love burning the leftovers," he says. "And there's the lathe." He points to the corner as he bends to add a piece of wood to the potbelly stove that's beside them.

Luke's space is a dream compared to the cubbyhole Vanessa has set up to work in next to the furnace at home. Each of the large north-facing windows has a view of the forest or the meadow, and there's a hook or a shelf for everything, including the many pieces of intricate gingerbread trim hanging to dry. But what really attracts Vanessa is the tidy mound of fresh sawdust and shavings in the corner of the shop. The mound looks like a nest to her.

"What's the pile for?" she asks.

"I'm building a path for the kids through the brush along the edge of the property. They love travelling through there."

"Aren't they lucky to grow up here. How many kids?"

"Two and one more on the way."

With this information, she is so inexplicably sad, she has no thought other than to get away.

"Great space, Luke. But look, I have to get going."

"Really? It's nasty and it's getting dark. You can wait it out here, if you like."

"I'm absolutely sure. I have to be back in Toronto before eight tonight."

"But you barely looked at the lathe."

"It's nice," she says. She doesn't know what words one is supposed to use when admiring a lathe. "Really. I have to go."

"Okay then. But be careful going over that cement slab at the river. It can be slippery when the weather's nasty."

She is so anxious to get going, she triggers the automatic button on her umbrella and gets hung up on the doorframe. She yards on it until one of the spines snaps and the fabric tears.

"Oh, too bad," Luke says.

"No worry. It's a cheap thing."

She scuttles across the yard knowing she looks like a humiliated sparrow with a broken pink wing flapping at her back. How could she have been so out of touch with the reality of this man's life? She's a middle-aged fool carrying a broken Italian designer umbrella.

The shame of it has her so hunched behind the wheel as she drives back down the road, she does not see the cement slab until she's skidding across it toward the far bank of the river. Her car moves sideways and lodges in the mud at the edge of the forest. She guns the engine and feels the car dig itself deeper. When she picks up her Blackberry, she sinks even further with the frustration of having no battery left. *Why the hell did I Google the directions to Slabtown so many times?* Impulsively, she crams the remnants of the chocolate donut she'd bought back in Toronto into her mouth. Then she drains the dregs of her coffee while she watches the last of the light in the sky disappear.

After a couple of hours sitting in the miserable, howling storm with not a single car passing by, she knows in her bones nobody will be coming or going on such a treacherous night. Her only option is to call on someone who lives in Slabtown to help.

The wind feels like it's going to take off the top of her head when she alights from the car. Within seconds, her umbrella blows inside out and lifts from her hand to lodge in the branches of an overhead oak. The armature hangs just out of reach like a small pink pterodactyl.

As she makes her way past the ghostly steel structure in front of the cathedral house, her coat's lining reaches the saturation point and she feels a wet slick move down her back. Water soaks her cerise sweater and camisole. She hammers on the door of the cathedral even though she knows no one is home. She is shivering by the time she circles the rammed-earth house, and has gone around it three times looking for a proper door before it dawns on her it's still under construction and nobody even lives there yet.

She is close to crying when she makes her way up the hill toward Luke's house. She creeps past his battered sign, now sunk in the mud, and across the lawn toward the front porch. She stops when she sees inside the brightly lit kitchen. There's a young girl, about seven or eight years old, sitting beside the toddler Vanessa had seen before. Luke is standing at the end of the table. They're all watching Shauna flip a pizza pie crust, laughing and cheering every time she throws it up and catches it. Somehow these successes clinch it for her. She cannot intrude on this perfect family.

Not knowing what else to do, she edges sideways in front of the window toward the workshop. When she reaches it, she pushes on the door and feels some relief as warm air hits her face. The potbelly stove has a few embers left from Luke's stoking. Still, it's dark but for the small glow from the stove, and she has to touch her way around the lathe and the drying racks toward the nest of shavings and sawdust. She peels off her wet coat to leave it on a stool near the fire, and hangs her sweater and camisole on an empty drying rack. She takes down Luke's work coat to wear while she shakes off the chill, and under the coat she finds his Hart House t-shirt. She pulls the shirt on, smelling him as the fabric passes over her nostrils.

Bundled into his clothing, she lies on his nest to breathe all of it in.

VANESSA ONLY INTENDED to stay long enough to warm up and give herself time to figure out what to do next. So after the embers die and the cold wakes her several hours later, she's startled to find she's been in a deep sleep in this intimate space. When she takes off Luke's coat and t-shirt, she thinks briefly about stuffing the shirt into her purse, but scolds herself for the thought. Still, she smells it once more before putting everything back. She rakes sawdust out of her hair with her fingers. Her own clothes are only slightly damp when she pushes open the door to check the yard, make sure no one is there. Then she skirts around the edge of the property back to the road and her car. It's cold and it's dark, but at least the wind and the rain have stopped.

After an hour sitting in her car, she watches the first light of morning come up. Everything seems less daunting, so she gives the backup one more try. But the wheels spin uselessly in the mud, and she is out on Slabtown Road, just starting to walk toward Beaver Valley Road, when she hears a vehicle coming behind her. She turns to see an old, red pickup driving down the hill. The truck stops beside her. Shauna and her daughter are inside it. Vanessa feels exposed and vulnerable in front of this woman, knowing she's spent a night wrapped in her husband's clothing, sleeping in his sanctuary without permission.

"Need some help?" Shauna asks.

"No, I'm good," Vanessa answers.

"Are you Luke's student from yesterday?"

Vanessa does her best to feign confusion, "Luke? No. I'm just waiting here for my husband."

"Are you sure? We can drive you out to the main road."

"No, I'm fine. I like the exercise. He'll be here soon."

Shauna stares at her as if to say, *Who do you think you're kidding?* And her daughter looks up at her with an expression that could be one of alarm or annoyance, it's difficult to tell. Eventually, after what feels like a lifetime of awkwardness, Shauna puts the truck in gear and drives off.

While Vanessa stands on the shoulder of Beaver Valley Road, she imagines the conversation Shauna will have later with Luke, how the two of them will try to piece together what had gone on. She is grateful when the second car that comes along picks her up and takes her to a garage where there's a tow truck.

The truck has an easy time pulling her car from the muck, but the driver isn't able to dislodge her pink umbrella from the oak tree.

"A marker from your visit," he chuckles.

LUCY IS BEYOND EXCITED the next week when she sees Vanessa carry the duffel bag of tools toward the car. The day is unusually warm for early December and when they pull up in front of the workshop, Vanessa thinks briefly about walking the park with Dick and Lucy instead of going inside.

"I really don't want to," she says.

"Why?" Dick asks.

"Some of the people are beginning to bug me. I'm glad it's almost over."

"It's the second last one. Go on. Have a good time." Dick plants a kiss on her lips, then adds, "Lucy and I will, won't we, old girl."

"Make sure she doesn't kill any ducks," Vanessa says as she gets out of the car.

"Are you kidding? After last week's performance, it's confirmed, the two of us are the worst duck hunters ever."

Vanessa is lacklustre in class, worried what Luke must think, what Shauna must have told him. Even more than usual, she avoids talking to anyone. But halfway through the session, Ernesto starts to go from bench to bench showing off his second box, the one lined in pink velvet. She's a little nervous what she might say if he gets to her. She has to consciously prepare not to tell him she thinks it's creepy how out of touch he is with today's standards.

He takes his time, sharing jokes and laughter with people as he goes, until he gets to Joe's bench. There, she hears him tell Joe, "She'll be eight in January, my princess." His eyes are gleaming and he wipes the back of his mouth with his hand as he says, "She's very bad with the leukemia now. I am only hoping my little angel makes it to her birthday." He does not come to Vanessa's bench. He walks instead to his own, where he sits on his stool and stares blankly.

Vanessa, feeling guilty and confused by her nasty thoughts, starts to slap on a second coat of varnish without waiting for the first to dry. Ernesto notices and comes over to her quietly. "Excuse me, lady. I don't mean to interfere, but you should wait until it's dry." He begins to wave his portable hairdryer over her box, helping her to speed the process.

She looks at him, sees the unhappy but friendly eyes, and wants to tell him she's so sorry about his princess, but she knows she wasn't supposed to hear what he'd said. Besides she's afraid she'll start to weep herself. When he shuts off the dryer, he says, "There. You take it home and give it one more good sand before you varnish again."

So it is with all the intention and understanding of grief that she gets into the car after class is finished and finds a grim-faced Dick.

"What is it?" she asks.

"It's Lucy. She ran off down at the pond. It took me a while to find her and when I did she was in the woods on the far side by the houses, and she couldn't walk very well."

Vanessa turns to look at Lucy in the back seat. She is very small and curled into an unnaturally tight position.

"Do you think she pulled something?"

"I don't know."

By the time they are fighting rush hour traffic across town, Lucy is only semi-conscious.

Dr. Purdy, the all-night vet, asks Vanessa and Dick to wait while he takes Lucy into the examination room. When he comes out after examining her, he sits in one of the waiting room chairs across from them.

"She drank antifreeze," he says.

"How could that happen?" Dick asks.

"Well, some guy realizes he hasn't changed his antifreeze in a year, and he takes advantage of this warm spell. He dumps pink liquid all over the driveway, goes inside to get more, and along comes Lucy who drinks up what tastes like lemonade to her."

Dr. Purdy folds his hands, lets this much settle in. Then he opens his hands to add, "She's going to die. We should euthanize her. Her kidneys have shut down. I'm sorry."

Vanessa is silent on the way home. How can she blame Dick? He's a good man, he loved Lucy more than she did. He's beating himself up a hundred times more than she is. And she's the bad person in all of this. She's the one who ran away to another man's nest, all Dick had done was take the dog for a walk. Yet somehow she does blame him. But for what? She's not sure.

"Where are you?" Dick asks.

The question startles Vanessa. "What do you mean?"

"You seem a million miles away."

"I don't know," she mutters. "I'm wandering in my mind."

At the next stoplight, Dick puts his hand on top of hers. "It's just you and me now. No wandering. Okay?"

Vanessa tries to smile, but only manages to make a strange half-whimper when she moves her lips.

LUKE BEGINS THE LAST CLASS with what sounds like the wrap-up.

"You've all done a fine job. It's been a pleasure working with you. I'm no good at goodbyes, so I'll just say bye for now. And I'll be here for the rest of today to help with individual finishing touches."

As soon as he stops talking, Vanessa can see Heather begin to move from workbench to workbench holding a badly concealed card that she's asking people to sign. She slinks lower and lower after each person, making it all the more obvious what she's doing. Vanessa is upset by the notion of it. She knows that the *thanks for everything* she'll scrawl at the bottom of the card is a pathetic understatement considering all that has gone on. To make up for it, when Heather asks for a small donation toward the gunsmith-style screwdrivers she's purchased as a parting gift, Vanessa hands her an over-generous $50. And she can't help but ask, "Really? Luke makes guns?"

"No, no," Heather whispers, "they're just very fine tools. They register best in the recesses."

After Heather tiptoes away, Vanessa looks down at her own box. She wants to line it like Ernesto had his. Not in pink velvet, but in blue satin. She's mad at herself for not listening when the process was explained, but she'd rather grow roots into the cement she's standing on than let her feet move forward to ask Luke for help. Instead, she slides over to Ernesto.

"I'd like to line my coffin … I mean my box. Can you help me?"

Ernesto let's out a friendly half-bawl of a laugh and says, "My lady, you will not fit in that box."

"Sorry," she laughs at her slip, "it's not my coffin. It's my dog's. She died last week."

"Oh, I'm terrible sorry, lady." It surprises her when he gives her a hug. He smells of ginger soap and toothpaste, not a hint of salami, red wine, garlic or espresso.

"It's Vanessa. I'm Vanessa. Hi," she says. She realizes how ridiculous this is, here it is the last class and she's introducing herself.

"I know, my beautiful lady. You are Vanessa."

Ernesto takes out one of the velvet panels in his box and shows her how it's covered and fitted into the lap edge. By the time he's helped make edges for Vanessa's box, it is fifteen minutes before the end of class. She can see Heather assembling the gift ready for presentation, so she thanks Ernesto then starts to quietly and efficiently assemble her tools. While Luke's back is turned to help a student at the front, she moves toward the exit. Ernesto follows.

He hands her a business card and whispers, "My son's restaurant. Bring your husband. We can talk about woodworking and I can help you with the lining if you need."

She smiles. "Thank you. Really, thank you for everything. We will come," she says. She means it.

ON THE WEEKEND Dick goes out to the plum tree in the backyard. The warm front has held, and he is wearing only a cardigan and a light pair of work pants while he clears away the remnants of a few rotted plums they hadn't harvested earlier in the fall. He begins to dig underneath the tree at the spot where Lucy liked to sleep on a hot summer's day. After a few minutes he turns and waves to Vanessa, who is waiting at the kitchen window. She comes and stands beside him.

"Are you sure? You worked hard. It's very nice," Dick says.

Together they look at the pine box that now holds Lucy. It's almost as if from the beginning she had made the box for their beloved furball. They'd told Dr Purdy a small lie, said they would bury Lucy immediately at Dick's brother's farm in Newmarket, didn't mention they'd be keeping her in the freezer chest so Vanessa would have time to make a satin lining.

Vanessa takes Dick's hand. "Yes, I'm sure. I'm going to build another one to put your beautiful tools in. I'll make it sacred from the beginning this time."

Dick digs one more layer down and they stand for a moment beside the grave.

"We have to work hard to let things go," Dick says.

He lifts the box into the hole and together they drop soil on top of it.

Gladiola Island

She watches as her silly hybrid rental car rocks between a decaying Econoline van and a dilapidated grey Toyota with spirit catchers hanging from every fastener. The van is so old it could have been on the last BC ferry she sailed, more than twenty-five years ago.

She is headed for what should be an island paradise at the top of the Georgia Strait. But Vanessa can only focus on whether it's going to be the murderer's van or the hippie's car that will scratch her rental. She breathes in. Breathes out. Tries to be mindful. Looks to the horizon for balance. For a moment all she can see is ocean rolling up to meet the sky. It should have liberated her.

The trip seemed like such a good idea, when she'd ducked into the organic grocers to wait out the pissing ice storm and spotted the Laurel Bush catalogues stacked beside the fresh raspberries. What could be better than a writers' retreat on Gladiola Island in the middle of August?

But as the weeks ticked down, and the Toronto weather got better, worries about her choice started to mount. *What if people think my writing is worse than Hallmark? (What if I think some of their cards are clever?) What if my room is unsleepable? Worse, what if I forget something essential?—even the catalogue warns 'no stores on the island'.*

The sight of the looming island makes her queasy, so Vanessa stops looking out and walks the decks instead. There's something a little off about the crowd. Some are just island folk, straw hats and mismatched wool socks give them away. And a few are families: a boy, a girl, a mom, a dad and various combinations. But a lot, like more than half, are couples, around her age, middle-aged or so, and mostly well-heeled. This is remarkable. Men don't usually go to writing workshops, especially not with their wives. When Vanessa finally spots another woman who seems to be on her own, she slows her pace to ask, "Are you headed to Laurel Bush?"

"Yes," the woman practically gushes, "for *Sharing the Heart Trail.* And you? Are you here with your hubby?"

Vanessa staggers a bit with the shift of the ferry, or perhaps it's the woman's response. Is she going to be navigating a horde of exploring couples? She would never have signed up if she'd known. Especially since the split with Dick has not gone that smoothly.

She ekes out a weak smile, "No. I'm going for a writing workshop."

"Oh," says the woman. "I didn't know they ran other courses this week."

"Me either."

Then for no reason Vanessa can fathom, the woman pushes her sunglasses up her nose and says, "You'll do fine."

THE TRUE GRAVITY of the situation does not sink in until the lithe little man at reception, the one who looks as if he could yoga himself into a pretzel, tells her, "There's unlimited herbal infusion and caffeine-free rooibos."

"And wine at dinner?" Vanessa asks.

Pretzel man makes a squishy little sound with his mouth before answering. "We seek an unobstructed experience for our guests."

A voice in her head screams, *You expect me to navigate this without cabernet?* She turns to see if she might find a different answer elsewhere in the room, and her knot of disappointment lands on the smiling, preppy couple registering in the line next to hers. The couple are fussing with multiples of Louis Vuitton luggage while being checked into an ocean front suite with private hot tub. So it hurts doubly when yoga pretzel man tells her, "Madam, you will be in the A-frame with shared facilities and a forest view."

"Ommmmmm," she chants as she drags her luggage toward the shack in the woods, the guest cart having been too full with Louis Vuitton to accommodate her. She's so absorbed in the task of simply getting to her cabin, she doesn't notice the majestic cedars, the wind eddying high in their branches, their lower boughs reaching down like welcoming arms. The only thing that keeps her going is the calming rhythm of the ocean behind her. She's just starting to relax about being at Laurel Bush when she arrives at her shack.

It's dismal. Nothing but two A-shaped squats joined in the middle by a bathroom. It needs paint and the walls shake when she unlocks her door. The bed in her room fills the entire space, and she has to use the Ommmmmm resonance in her throat to manoeuver around it, to get to the communal hall and shared bathroom. Once there, the bathroom door bangs shut and the walls shake again. In a small fury of need, she unpacks her toiletries, covering most of the convenient shelf and counter space, and as she does, she makes up her mind that no matter how quiet the people in the adjoining squat turn out to be, she will hate them forever if they wake her even once with a dropped tube of toothpaste or an over-enthusiastic midnight pee. She is absolutely certain about this, just as certain as she is that no quantity of herbal infusion or caffeine-free rooibos will be able to do anything about it.

When she exits the bathroom, she walks to the end of the hall and peeks behind the door which has been left open into her cabin mate's side of the structure. A purple, crushed velvet dress is draped over a suitcase abandoned in the middle of the floor—its contents a jumble of different coloured velvet dresses and sensible sandals. *Good, it's not a wandering couple*, she thinks.

THE FIRST TIME Vanessa smiles is at the communal dinner table when Sandy, a fifty-something-year-old man dressed in a Lacoste golf shirt and surfer jams, picks up his registration material and reads aloud the description of *Sharing the Heart Trail.* He stops after the words *to learn the spiritual and inner connectedness that will lead to deeper emotional and physical commitment* to say, "Oh god, Lisbeth, you had us drive all the way from Southern California for this? It sounds like so much bullshit."

"Thank you for that," Vanessa laughs.

Lisbeth, who is so anorexically thin that her floor length tie-dye t-shirt and silver hoop earrings look like they might drag her into the depths of the earth, pushes a piece of kale around her plate and asks, "Thank you for what?"

"Sandy's honesty," Vanessa answers.

Lisbeth is clearly displeased, and makes no response other than to swoop up her and Sandy's plates. Vanessa watches as she glides over the beautiful strawberry-blonde fir floor toward the clean-up bins, where she begins the process—food scraps into the slop, napkins to recycling, cutlery separated from the plates, each dipped into its own tub of ginger-scented water.

"Well, enjoy your evening session," Sandy says, as he stands to follow Lisbeth. When he moves from the table, Vanessa hears a sound like, "Grrrrump." She can't tell whether it's directed at her, but suspects it might be.

After she clears and sorts her own dishes, she shuffles shoeless across the floor to the rack of cubbyholes where footwear is stored during meals. She shoves her feet into her running shoes and starts up the wood chip path to Cedar House, the place where her group will be meeting. The ice in her glass of lemon infusion tinkles when yoga pretzel man from reception stops her.

"Please, no glassware outside the dining hall. We provide hot and cold thermal mugs for sale in the gift shop."

"Okay. I'll remember for next time," she says, and carries on up the path with glass in hand.

The group seated at the long table inside Cedar House is only ten, a much better size than the mass of couples. The leader who sits at the head of the table, and whose catalogue picture resembled the Maharishi, turns out in real life to look more like an Anglican minister. As if by secret code no one talks, waiting for the minister to decide when. A full five minutes after the start time, his lips begin to move.

"Greetings. My name is Nigel. I'll be the leader for your *Profound Writing*." He pauses to let the profoundness of what he's about to say be silently announced. "You're all trying to vanish into your work, when what you really need is to find the space to do it in. Before we introduce ourselves, I want to begin with the simple, silent affirmation: *I can do this. I am ready*. Close your eyes and feel it in your core."

The curly-haired young man to Vanessa's left, one of two men in the group, repeats the affirmation loudly. "I CAN do this. I AM ready."

Nigel peers down the centre of the table. "Silently," he says. "Try to stay in the trance of creativity."

Vanessa can't make the affirmation at all. Instead she is thinking, *I can't do this. I'm not in the mood.* She looks across the table at a round woman in her sixties. *At least ten years older than I am. That's what I would look like if I let myself go.* The woman is wearing the deep purple crushed velvet that had been draped over the suitcase in the other squat of the cabin. She seems sort of folded in half, almost asleep. Vanessa wonders what she is thinking.

When the trance of creativity has stretched almost to the snapping point, Nigel asks everyone to say *just a little* about their writing. Most are vague, say things like *have been writing for a long time, started in high school, picked it up again recently,* including crushed velvet cabin mate who turns out to be named Kathy and is *into poetry.*

Vanessa is relieved there appear to be only two pros in the group. One is a pretty lifestyle reporter for CTV named Jill. Nigel diagnoses her as needing to *shatter her seriousness.* And the other is a strong-boned, first-time novelist named Barbara who doubts she can write another novel. Nigel tells Barbara to *find the fun in the writing again.*

After Vanessa introduces herself, mumbling something about *hoping to write a decent poem one day*, Nigel's one-second diagnosis for her is *get over your disappointment.* She doesn't remember saying anything about being disappointed, but there it is, pronounced in such a way she knows she's not supposed to argue.

Nigel ends the evening with, "Let meaning trump mood. You do not need to be in the right mood to write. And everybody please listen for the barred owl on the way back to your cabin. He's the one hooting *Who-cooks-for-you*?"

She follows the tiny beam of her flashlight down the path toward the A-frame. She keeps some distance behind Kathy. She's not ready to introduce herself, and she's feeling guilty about spreading her stuff around the bathroom, especially after Kathy told the group she's recovering from some unspecified illness and needs writing to *find herself again.* Nigel had told her to *coddle the fragile egg.*

Vanessa wakes in the middle of the night to hear the barred owl's hoot. She feels a little sad she has no answer other than *nobody*.

AT BREAKFAST, she finds an empty table in the corner away from the windows. Most of the couples are clambering for seats with ocean views, and she can't locate any of the writers in the sea of faces. She is content to sit on her own, but halfway through her bowl of granola and hemp hearts, a couple of women with matching haircuts, matching hairbands, matching glasses—in fact, matching everything except one is in a wheelchair and has an assist dog—begin to make their way toward the table. Vanessa, unsure how to assimilate all this information, keeps her eye on her bowl, but soon feels the dog by her feet, and hears the sound of a chair being moved away so the wheelchair can pull up.

"Hi. I'm Donna, and this is my partner Sarah. The dog is Megabyte. Mind if we join you?"

"Not at all," Vanessa says as she puts her hand down to pat Megabyte, who promptly licks her fingers, making it impossible for her to continue eating with that hand.

"Are you here with a partner?" Donna asks.

"No, I'm here for a writers' course."

"Oh, how great. I've always wanted to be a writer," Sarah says. "What have you published that I might have read?"

This feels like the most personal and defeating question that could have been put to her, and for one millisecond Vanessa is tempted to ask, *And what bed death experience are you here to work out?* Instead she smiles and says, "I'm just a beginning writer."

Everyone looks uncomfortable with that answer and, as soon as she can without being rude, she rises from her chair. "Got lots to do. See you all later." She moves toward the sanitation station, and then the drink station to fill her expensive new thermal mug with rooibos.

Three-quarters of the group are already gathered at Cedar House by the time she sits down. Nigel has not yet arrived, but Kathy her cabin mate, who is wearing dark green crushed velvet this morning, speaks up.

"Is anybody else finding this place irritating? Someone on the other side of my cabin snores and visits the washroom all night long."

Vanessa tips her head down and is glad she hasn't yet introduced herself. She'd tried not to pee so often during the night, but she'd drunk too much herbal infusion hoping it might make some sort of happy substitute. And although toward the end of their marriage Dick had begun to mention she snored, she never really believed it until this very second.

Only the curly-haired young man, whose name Vanessa has already forgotten, engages Kathy. "You better change rooms," he says.

"Who is changing rooms?" Nigel asks as he enters from the ocean-side deck. "What an incredible view we have out here."

"I am," says Kathy. "I'll be back right after I arrange it with reception."

Kathy gathers up her multiple notebooks, her colour-coded pens, her laptop, and exits.

As soon as she's out of earshot, Nigel says, "I wonder if she's coming back?"

No one responds, so Nigel continues. "Well if she doesn't, keep in mind she was here for a reason. Possibly to give one of us a lesson. Okay, today's headline is *choose and commit.* I want you to reflect on this. If you've already chosen what you're going to write this week, go do it now. If you're having trouble, write a synopsis of two or three things, then commit to one. Go for thirty minutes."

People scatter. Vanessa walks with her empty notebook to the far end of the yard. She sits in a plastic chair and stares into a tangle of blackberry bushes just coming on ripe. *This is bogus*, she thinks. *I've spent a thousand dollars to have someone utter less than a hundred words per hour, while I sit in a place less comfortable than my own home and still don't write.* She can hear the woman named Alicia somewhere behind her talking non-stop. When she turns to find out to whom she's speaking, she sees Alicia is alone at the picnic table and appears to be talking to her computer.

Vanessa pulls out her Blackberry to check the time, but starts checking and rechecking emails, as if commanding one more search is going to turn up something more interesting than a renewal notice from an online magazine she never subscribed to, or another proposition from Svetlana who thinks she's a lonely old man. After more than fifteen minutes have passed and nothing new has appeared on her screen, she begins to scribble in her journal. She writes a title, *Under the Bell Jar.* It's to be a poem about her marriage. The only other words she writes on that page are *trapped from the beginning.*

She flips to another page and writes a new title, *Spring Breakup.* Almost immediately a number of lines come to her.

Every year it's a surprise
when the ice goes out
the year father went down
up to his waist
we laughed
the crack
the fish floating belly up
it was nothing
everyone survived
except the fish
until the year the water split
at the seam

split at the seam
and they drowned
the wild iris blooming
at the edge of the stream
we won't pick the iris
ever again

She looks at the page and thinks there may be something here.

For the first time since arriving at Laurel Bush, she feels a little excited. She's got something she wants to try out on the group. See what they think of the beginning of her poem.

"Time," Nigel calls from the deck.

Once everyone is assembled back in the room, Nigel asks, "What did you learn about your writing?"

Alicia pushes a button on her computer and it begins to talk, reciting words to the group in an Alicia-cyber-altered-voice.

"Stop," Nigel says. "What is that?"

"It's Dragon Maker," she says. "Voice-activated software."

"Okay. On your own time, Alicia. We're not here to workshop people's writing. We're here to explore the writing experience itself."

This is news to Vanessa. She thought it was a writing workshop, and she's not the only one who's confused. When Nigel asks again, "What did you learn?" Jill the CTV reporter says, "I'm writing a memoir about travelling and depression, and I'd like to share a few lines about my family…"

"Stop," Nigel says. "We are here to learn about the process of writing, not to hear what you are in fact writing."

Only the curly-haired young man seems to get it. He puts his hand up and when Nigel nods, he says, "I learned writing can be meditative if you trust. I free wrote without critiquing on two different myths, and when I finished I realized only one was worth committing to."

"Thank you, Stephen," Nigel says. "A writer's biggest challenge is to choose and commit. The next story not yet written always seems more sparkly than the one for which you have started to put serious words on the page."

Nigel doesn't ask again what any of us learned, instead he says, "Okay. Back out to write some more. If you still haven't committed, that's your challenge. If you have, then go deeper. Go for forty-five minutes."

By the time Vanessa is walking back for the morning wrap-up, she's beginning to understand what Nigel has been telling them. She did go deeper with *Spring Breakup* and now it's a mess; she actively has to resist moving back to *Under the Bell Jar.* It looks so much more sparkly with only four words scribbled under the title. The struggle to commit is tiring.

AT LUNCH VANESSA carries a tray with organic leek soup and beet salad to the end of one of two quaint wooden tables nestled under the apple tree outside the dining hall. She cannot face the hall right now, and the tree is like a beacon calling *sanctuary* to her. Seated at the other table are a young Asian couple and an older bearded man whose facial hair looks like it's been knit to his face. The beard looks up at Vanessa and says, "We're in deep session right now."

"Excuse me?" Vanessa answers.

"I should explain," he says. "I am one of the counsellors with the couples' group and we are in session here."

Vanessa's mind screams. *I paid my money too. Just because these people messed up their marriage doesn't mean you get to take the prime eating spot. My marriage screwed up too.* Instead she says a simple, "Okay."

Knit-beard speaks again, "Thank you for understanding. My

name is Joshua. Perhaps we'll meet again under lighter circumstances. Embrace your afternoon."

The young bride, who has been making utterances like an injured bird throughout Joshua's sweetness and light departure speech, lets out a sad, "So sorry," when Vanessa picks up her tray to move on.

She walks toward the dining hall. At the door she passes Alicia, who is embracing a young woman adorned in crystals. She hears Alicia say, "Thank you for letting me share the adventure of my life." Vanessa imagines what the words would sound like in a Dragon-cyber-voice.

By the time she finally sets her tray down in the dining room, the soup has scummed over. She picks at the beets and fennel on her plate, but decides to join the dessert line instead. The line is long, but the sight of lemon pie at the end picks up her spirits, until the chubby, older woman ahead of her begins to motion for her husband to come forward. "Morris. Morris. Get up here. We'll be late for the afternoon if you don't budge in."

Morris's look announces he'll be in for it if he doesn't do as commanded, so he slips in front of Vanessa, a sheepish grin on his face. This endears him to her so she asks, "How's it going in your group?"

"Oh, it's all very interesting," he says.

"Do you have to be part of a couple to join?"

"Yes. But some of them are not doing so well. Some are…" Morris lowers his voice as if he's sharing a secret, "… some are even the same sex."

"Morris!" his wife thumps his chest. "Not doing well and same sex are not synonymous."

"I know sweetheart. I'm just saying." Chagrined, he turns away from Vanessa for the remainder of their inch-forward toward dessert.

She leaves the dessert table feeling jilted, her slice of lemon pie jiggling.

"THE HEADLINE this afternoon is *use only words that serve you.* What do I mean by this?"

Nigel asks rhetorically, but RainDear, the red-headed organic farmer from Belleville doesn't catch the drift. She starts to answer.

"I'll share an anecdote of something I learned during light therapy about the power of full spectrum to reinforce the body's service."

"I'd love to hear about that," Alicia encourages.

"No, let's not pursue this," Nigel says, "otherwise we'll spend all our time on it. What I want you to keep in mind this afternoon is that even if your mind tells you *this is a mess*, it's your job to love it. Your words to yourself should be *this writing is meaningful to me.* And if you have not committed yet, to commit is your foremost job. Now go, write for forty-five and come back committed."

Vanessa heads for her chair at the back of the yard, but is beat out by Alicia who is already there setting up Dragon central. She's tempted to find another chair and pull it nearby so she can sit and stare into the blackberries, until she hears Dragon repeating back, "The horse throbs wildly under my thighs." *No wonder Nigel doesn't want us to share*, she thinks.

She settles at the edge of the deck instead and stares out into the ocean until she feels compelled to scribble a few more desolate words in her journal about the spring breakup. After a time the lines she writes begin to blur into breakups in general. The words she loves the most—*the moon hangs like a bruised plum in the sky/ how dare he do this to me*—these words don't seem to fit into either of the poems she's started. They're not wedded to anything. Besides she's the one who left Dick, so maybe these words belong to another poem, another life even.

"Writing tools down," Nigel calls.

Vanessa is close to crying when she sits back at the table. She had not expected so many thoughts about breakups to surface at the workshop.

Nigel begins with, "Realize that whenever anyone finds out you are a writer, the next question will be, What are you writing about? Shut that one down as quickly as possible. It will suck the life out of you if you talk too much about your writing. And really, nobody cares. Why is that? It's because most people believe they are going to be writers too, and they just want to pick your brains."

Stephen begins to speak holding his hand high, "But is it okay for us to say we are writers?"

"Of course it is," Nigel says. "That's why you're all here, isn't it? To go deeper. To say a simple *I am a writer* will serve you well. Relax man, arms at your side."

Stephen grins and puts his hand down.

"Okay," Nigel says, "we'll go around the room and all of you give a one-liner as to what you're writing about, then I'll say, Tell me more, and you give me your exit line from the conversation."

Nigel starts with Stephen, which means Vanessa will be asked last. At first she likes this until she realizes as they go around all the good shutdown lines are disappearing. She especially likes the novelist Barbara's line, "I don't want to talk about it too much, it will let the air out of the tires." And the weaver Trixie's line, "I'm too superstitious to talk about it, the prince of darkness might be listening."

So by the time Nigel gets to Vanessa, her heart is pounding and her mind is almost blank. She stammers, "I'm not really sure what I'm writing. I've started a bunch of poems that are all running together and nothing is jelling."

"Hmmm," Nigel says. "Tell me more."

"Well, I hope you'll get to read one of my poems someday."

Nigel looks at her with lips moving like a lizard in advance of his words, then finally he says, "Sounds kind of snarky."

Vanessa is stunned. He'd responded to all the others with positive words, or with nothing at all but an encouraging smile. Her dry run was the lone one to have garnered a big thumbs down, and she's left completely unclear how *snarky* fits with the philosophy of using only words that will serve her well.

Her heart starts to hammer in her ears and she is conscious that her face is turning purple with hormonal stress. For the rest of the afternoon, she doesn't hear most of what Nigel has to say until she becomes aware everyone else is packing up. She follows on autopilot to the door, and is about to exit when Nigel says, "It's apparent to me, Vanessa, that you have not yet committed. This evening it is your task to commit." He pronounces the last word with a great flourishing point at her, like his is the finger of God.

THE NAKED PAINTER on the beach helps Vanessa find wine on the island. She had not realized she'd wandered off the property and was on private land until the man popped up from between two logs with a canvas in his hand and a streak of navy paint on his upper thigh.

"Ahoy," he says. "Can I help you?"

"I was out for a walk, didn't realize you were here."

"No, of course you wouldn't. Are you from the Bush?"

"You mean Laurel Bush?"

"Yeah. Their property ends a few hundred feet back, but lots of folks end up here."

"Oh, I thought they owned the whole point."

"No. They just behave like they do. The property stops at the laurel hedge."

"I don't even know what laurel looks like."

"It's that shiny green leaf bush you see at the edge of their property. Not that much to look at really. Sort of a weed if you ask me. But how are you enjoying it?"

Vanessa is having trouble juggling the conversation while maintaining appropriate eye contact. The man, who is about her age, is obviously an accomplished nudist. He carries on his side of the chat as if there's nothing unusual about his appearance. Her gaze keeps drifting around his surprisingly fit anatomy, from right nipple to left, down centre hair line to navel, then on to occasional collision with scrotum and attachment, and back up to navel. She wishes she were wearing sunglasses because she knows her eyeballs are popping. She hears herself answer, "It's okay, but I'm dying for some wine. They should have told us there was no alcohol on the island."

The man laughs, "You need to come to the Spa."

"Excuse me?"

"Regulars at the Bush know all about it. Come with me."

He crooks his finger as he heads down an overgrown trail leading from the beach toward a ramshackle cottage. She feels vulnerable following him, but she keeps saying to herself, *commit, commit.* When they get to the porch he turns to ask, "What do you want, honey? Smokes, pot or alcohol?"

"Oh I get it. Spa. Clever. Do you have any cabernet?"

"No, honey. Only white table wine this week. It goes good with the homegrown, though. Can sell you some wine plus a couple of joints for thirty bucks—this week's special."

"I haven't smoked pot in years …"

"Well time you did again," the man laughs.

Vanessa stares. She knows she needs to respond and not knowing how to be around the offer of pot, but knowing she would really like the wine, she says, "Sure, I'll take the special, but I'll need somebody to share the pot with. I don't really remember how to do it."

"That's a good deal for me. I'll spark one up with you, honey."

He begins to fuss with the pillows on one of the cedar porch chairs. He points to the chair and says, "Take a load off."

Vanessa is distinctly uncomfortable with the notion of sitting down, but once seated, she realizes it's better than standing because she can face away from his nether region and not appear to be rude. She wonders why she is so uncomfortable, it's not as if she hasn't been around naked men before. He disappears inside, and when he returns with a joint and a lighter along with a carton of white wine, she notices a tiny diamond stud glinting in one ear. She doesn't know what to make of it. It's sort of compelling, but sleazy at the same time. Possibly it means he's gay. Though that thought is a little disappointing. All his enthusiastic smiles and honey endearments might just be affectations.

He puts the wine at her feet, sits in the other chair, lights the joint, and hands it to her. Predictably, she coughs out the first toke before it's halfway down her windpipe.

"Easy sister," he laughs. "Try that again with a little less enthusiasm."

She manages to keep the next couple of tokes down, but by the time the joint comes by a fourth time, a fearful-paranoid-dead-head feeling has descended. It reminds her why she gave up smoking years earlier, when she'd moved back to Toronto after her hippie time living in Victoria.

"That's it for me," she says.

"Okay. I'll put this puppy out," he jumps to his feet. "Wrap the rest in foil for you."

She trembles with paranoia as she waves her hand no, but he's not paying attention. He disappears inside and is back in a flash with the joint in a piece of foil that looks like a crushed minnow. Her feet have to get moving and there's no time to argue about it, so she shoves the small dead fish into her pocket, picks up the wine and races down the path toward the beach.

"Quicker to take the road out front, sister," he calls. "Come visit anytime."

BACK ON THE COMPOUND, stinking of pot and carrying a box of wine, Vanessa runs into yoga pretzel man from reception. His words *we seek an unobstructed experience for our guests* float in her mind, and she starts to giggle. At least she's on to the part of smoking pot that she likes, the part where paranoia is replaced with a sense that everything is grandly amusing.

"Good evening, madam," pretzel man says.

"It is," she answers, hoisting the wine toward him before continuing her sideways drift toward the A-frame. Once there, she flings open the door and glides into the common hall toward the bathroom in search of a drinking vessel. At the end of the hall, she notices the door to Kathy's room is wide open again. The room is vacant and made-up, ready for the next guest. Vanessa is definitely on the pot roller coaster now because she suddenly feels sad. Kathy never did return to the workshop and Vanessa starts to think she'd been there to teach her not to be selfish, to be more forgiving, to stop looking down her nose at people. In short, to learn to fit in. *Oh god. I'm not fitting in. I'm the only one that Nigel thinks is snarky. But I'm horny and I want to have sex with ____? hmmm, what's his name? the nude painter.*

This last thought stops the roller coaster for a moment. The car she's sitting in shudders at the notion of having sex and the fact her mind slotted the naked artist into the blank is crazy. She hadn't even figured that out when she was staring at the real thing. All of that flesh. How much more obvious does it need to be?

Her car swings with the momentum of the roller coaster starting up again, and for a second it turns to the ecstatic when she focuses on having the entire space to herself. She does a grateful fairy twirl in the hall outside the bathroom, then closes the door to the other side, feeling exposed as if in fact somebody has already checked-in and she just isn't seeing them.

She sits on her bed and takes the sanitary wrap from the plastic glass. Fitting, she's about to drink heavily fortified wine from a shatterproof container.

After a second glass, she thinks the roller coaster might be slowing down as she drifts into happy memories of being a twenty-five-year-old living in Victoria, a young fashion designer dating fishermen and loggers. But then at the edge of the memory is one that eventually lurches everything to a stop, giving her a clear view of the disaster that was Jake—the Victoria bass player who carried a quiver of instruments and the musty smell of sex everywhere he went. The way he had ended things with her. Heartbreaking. But evidently thoughts of the smell of Jake can still settle inside her and make her uterus stand on end.

She gulps a third glass of wine, and when she finally slams the door on the roller coaster, she feels sufficiently girded to tackle the communal dining experience.

She carries a tray of organic Bengali dinner to the arm of an Adirondack beside the table at the end of the deck. Joshua the knit-beard is at the table in deep session again. He's talking with an over-tall, over-married man sitting next to a pretty but sullen wife. She keeps swiping the end of her twitching nose with the sleeve of her sweater. Vanessa has had enough wine not to care that she is eavesdropping, and Joshua seems to have given up on the privacy thing.

She hears Joshua say, "We all get overwhelmed sometimes. One minute my wife is a Jewish princess, the next she's a goddess. I wait for the goddess moments."

"I do too," over-tall says. "But those moments aren't coming clear to me. To be honest, we aren't getting much out of this workshop. Are their any toolboxes we can take home with us?"

At this, Vanessa turns her back a little out of respect for the awkward young man. But she can still hear everything.

"There are no toolboxes," Joshua says. "Work on one thing at a time. That's the best advice I can give." Joshua stands ready to leave, then perhaps recognizing he needs to do a bit of PR, he adds, "Watching you two work on the exercises this morning was beautiful."

After Joshua moves toward another couple, the pretty, rabbit-nose wife asks over-tall, "What do you take from that?"

"To make conversations just conversations, nothing more. To diffuse. To not feed the fire."

Neither of them says anything more and after a moment of awkward silence, a moment when even Vanessa can't swallow her food, they depart. The wife glowers, her embers clearly waiting to be fed. Vanessa aligns with her, and yet she does not want to be her. She feels sorry for over-tall, and half-inclined to jump up and warn him, *She's going to leave you.*

Alone on the deck, she has a moment of feeling sorry for Dick. She'd been that angry wife toward the end. She'd infused everything with hostile silence. He'd tried at least to douse the irritated fire. She could have worked herself into a sentimental, overwrought state except that Nigel sits down beside her at the place where over-tall had been sitting, and shows Vanessa a bowl of cardamom rice pudding.

"This is good," he says. "My second."

"I haven't had any yet."

She is pleased they might have a real conversation, until out of the corner of her eye, she sees a flush-faced man whose nose looks like it's going to consume his face. The man is moving toward them. When he gets to the table, he plunks himself across from Nigel.

"I hear you're the leader of the writing group. I'd love to join the group next year. But I'm here with the wife this time."

"Yes," Nigel says.

She senses Nigel is getting ready to shut down a conversation which seems headed toward writing. But so far, the man is undaunted by the initial monosyllabic answer. She waits for the exit line.

"What do you talk about in the group?" the man asks.

"Writing," Nigel says. "Tell me about your writing?"

Bingo. It works. The man completely abandons his questions and starts with what Vanessa knows is going to be a very long tale beginning with, "Well I have quite a unique story. After I lost my license to practice medicine, I descended into the bottle for a time, but I resurfaced to find …"

As she picks up her tray, Nigel interrupts the man to speak to her, "Have a good evening, Vanessa. Don't forget to work on committing."

NEXT MORNING Vanessa is exhausted. All night she kept waking with dry mouth, not from the wine, although that probably didn't help, but from too many disturbed dreams about unachieved sexual experiences in which both Jake with his standup bass and the naked artist featured prominently. She knows it's symbolic of her inability to commit, and is lying irritated with the thought of it when she hears the morning triangle ring outside the dining hall. While she dresses, she wonders whether the sound makes anybody else resonate with an association to the TV show *Bonanza*—it seems so incongruous with the otherwise new-ageness of the Laurel Bush Centre.

In the dining hall, she waits at the tea stand behind red-headed RainDear from the writing group. RainDear is engaged in a hug with a plump woman not from the group, the two of them embracing, eyes closed, hands moving slowly and lovingly in small circles up and down each others backs. They end with a wrap-up tussle and a satisfied *emmhhh,* followed by another vaguely sexual sound. Then just as they appear to be finished, they go at it again. Vanessa realizes she must have been staring because when they finally do finish, RainDear asks, "Want an omega hug, Vanessa?"

"Oh no thanks, just woke up."

"Okay. Celebrate your day."

Vanessa fills her thermal mug with rooibos and heads toward Cedar House. She can't face steel-cut oat pancakes after hearing her day is to be celebrated. Especially not with a hangover.

Alone in the yard she pulls out her journal and stares at it. She's written nothing but chicken scratch and dog's breakfast since arriving. It's hard to commit to either one, especially when most of the others in the group seem to have already finished at least half a manuscript of publishable quality. She's wondering, *What's wrong with me?* when Nigel calls out, "Everybody. Come on in."

He begins the morning session with, "We all need to get over our own personalities. They get in the way of writing. If you let your personality intrude, even if you block a week off to come away to a retreat, you won't write. You will end up having an affair instead."

"Not if you come on the same week as the couples," young

Stephen quips.

Everyone laughs and Vanessa waits for Nigel to shut it all down. She's surprised when instead he lets Alicia tell an over-long story about her penchant for home decorating, which everyone hopes will somehow end in a tale of an affair, but ends with her saying, "I think my obsession with candles is a good example of what you mean about personality getting in the way of writing."

Then Nigel, perhaps out of a sense of fairness, goes around the room and asks everyone what it is they think gets in the way of their writing. The excuses range from the banal—taking care of the dog, the baby, the garden—to the strikingly unusual from the quiet, bald man, who issues a showstopper when he says, "My obsession with guns."

Even Nigel doesn't know what to say except, "Still waters run deep, brother."

When it's Vanessa's turn, she's flustered and wants to say to the quiet bald man, *Get away.* Instead she says, "I don't know. But something's stopping me. I haven't really written anything all week."

Nigel looks at her, "You know what's stopping you."

"Inability to commit?" she replies.

"And that's because …"

"I'm afraid."

She surprises herself. She never admits to fear. Never, ever.

"Of what?" Nigel asks. "You don't have to tell us. But think about it. What are you afraid of?"

Vanessa stares at Nigel. She hopes her expression looks impassive, but from the inside of her skull she knows there's a rapid succession of blinks going on that are commands to self to not cry.

"Now everybody go," Nigel says. "Put your personalities aside and write acutely for an hour and a half. We'll meet back here just before lunch and see what progress has been made."

Vanessa sits in the yard and writes the word FEAR in the middle of the page. She draws a box around it and stares at it for half an hour. Then she writes the word FRAUD underneath it. Even Beethoven could get his difficult personality out of the way to write beautiful symphonies. Why can't she, for just one second? She can't stand how stuck she feels.

SOMETHING IS DIFFERENT about the couples at lunch. A lot more of them are holding hands. Vanessa wonders if this is for show, whether each couple, afraid to look weaker than the other, is holding hands in a show of coupledom?—or has some miracle been worked on the group? Even the young Asian bride, who had fluttered like a bird when Vanessa interrupted her counselling session under the apple tree, is sitting happily with her husband who keeps his arm around her shoulder. Only the over-tall, over-married man with the pretty wife and her twitching, rabbit nose look awkward. He holds her purse while she pokes at her chile relleno.

Midway through the meal, Joshua the knit-beard rises to introduce his wife Paula, who has a microphone in her hand.

"We have had an incredible morning," Paula says. "Everybody has worked hard, beginning with an anger management session where we yelled and yelled, to get all the aggression out. And now everybody feels so much better. Right?"

All the couples, except for over-married and rabbit nose, clap and cheer. Megabyte barks from under a table somewhere.

"Oh yes, who can forget Megabyte? He got the most upset with all the yelling and showed us dogs are less inured to anger than people. But after our anger, we healed through dance. So Joshua, Megabyte and I want to invite everybody at Laurel Bush to join us in a celebration circle of healing dance."

Stevie Wonder's *You Are the Sunshine of My Life*, a song that

Vanessa had liked up until this moment, begins to play. Megabyte is first out. He circles the wheelchair in time to Stevie, while the others flood the floor. Vanessa follows over-tall and his wife out of the dining room. She walks three paces ahead of him. He still carries her purse.

In the glare of the sun, Vanessa's not sure what to do with herself except to get the hell away from the dining hall. The upcoming afternoon is meant to be unstructured, so she can dive into her writing, really push it. But since there's nothing to push she wanders generally in the direction of the gift shop. She is leafing through the Laurel Bush cookbook searching for the ginger sesame recipe when Sandy, who's come from South California with Lisbeth, and has doffed his surfer jams and Lacoste shirt in favour of a hemp manskirt and Birkenstocks, glides into the shop and heads toward the far bookcase. He stops under the sign *Sexuality and Relationships*. He has that same ecstatic look on his face that most of the couples seem to have now, so he too must have drunk the Kool-Aid. For several minutes, he is intently buried in a book with a red and gold binding. When he's finished, he shoves the book back into its space with a slight self-satisfied grunt, then glides back out of the shop.

Vanessa waits a minute to be sure he won't return. She strolls over to pluck the red and gold book with the title *Rapture* from the shelf, and opens it randomly. Although it's hard to describe what she is looking at, the words *full throbbing penis* come to mind. She thumbs through several pages until she spontaneously snaps the book shut after lighting on the page that illustrates the proper way to insert Ben Wa balls into the woman's vagina. She leaves the shop with images in her head of Sandy in full battle attire, dangling Ben Wa balls from his fingertips, and follows her feet back to the A-frame, where she unwraps the shatterproof glass in the bathroom and pours out the remainder of the wine from the box.

VANESSA WAKES the morning of the last full day of workshop and bypasses breakfast all together. She can see a large number of couples on the porch of the dining room looking too much like they're waiting out a set break at a dance hall. Instead of venturing near, she goes around the building and tries to sneak through the kitchen in an attempt to access rooibos from the rear.

Yoga pretzel man catches her. "Madam this area is private. Can I assist?"

"Yes. You can. You can find me some coffee."

"Brewed coffee is for sale every morning until 10 in the gift shop, Madam."

"Really? How come no one told me this before? This place is messed up."

She is surprised how happy this snap makes her feel. Even pretzel man's wan, beatific smile doesn't take the pleasure away from it.

When she arrives at the gift shop, she snatches the red and gold *Rapture* from the bookshelf and pushes it toward the young, female clerk, who is dressed in the sheerest of sheer cotton dress, and says, "Plus a large coffee to go please."

"Okay. Cream?"

"No thanks, black."

The clerk gives her another beatific smile, as if to say, *I hope you find the same enlightened path that I'm on without stimulants.* But no matter, the coffee is soon coursing through Vanessa's veins, picking up her day as she walks toward Cedar House.

Nigel begins the morning session with, "Fear makes us fuck up. Apocalyptic thinking is ancient, resurgent and wrong. Things are generally better than we believe and we must access our innate joy to really write down what it is we have to say."

He stands at the head of the table in sermon position, while Vanessa sips coffee. She feels her heart palpitate when he raises his hands above the group, his gesture so like a blessing. "Today we will banish fear and find the ritual that works for each of us."

She thinks she's found the ritual. Coffee. But when she's staring down the bottom of her cup, she hasn't had enough. She excuses herself and rises from the table to rush back down the path to the gift shop before the last of it disappears for the day. She orders four cups, "For the group," she says, and scuttles back to the A-frame where she leaves three behind for later. She slips back into the workshop in time to hear Nigel say, "To banish the fear you need to courageously notice what's going on. Sometimes it's just that kick-the-shit-out-of-yourself feeling that helps you find a courageous affirmation to carry on."

"Flip the magnet," Jill says.

Everyone nods gravely.

Vanessa knows she's missed some important attraction-repulsion metaphor while out scrounging for coffee. She's formulating a question when Nigel interrupts her thought with, "Rituals. What we're hunting down here, Vanessa, is a ritual that will help keep us going. Each of you take a sheet of paper and quickly write on it one *should not*. Then we'll read it and rip it up. Go."

Vanessa is unsure why this has to be done with such urgency and is anxious about all that she has missed while out of the room, including what exactly a *should not* is. But she knows an inquiry is not going to be well received, so she scribbles a few words on a tiny piece of paper and puts it in front of herself with her hand over it. Nigel looks down at her hand but speaks instead to Barbara.

"You had some big doubts when we started, Barbara, about your ability to write another novel. We'll start with you as I sense you have a considerable *should not.*"

Barbara smiles and starts to read, "I should not have quit writing to put Glen through architecture school, and then once he was finished, I should not have let the bastard stay in the house."

"Bravo," Nigel says. "The start of a novel!"

And on it goes around the table—*I should not have let my family talk me out of being the wonderful writer I know I am, I should not have had so many sexual distractions, I should not have remained celibate for so long, I should not have wasted so much time seeking attention.*

When it comes to Vanessa, she takes her hand off the paper and has to pick it up to read it because the script is so small. "I should not think I am too old to start writing."

"Well done everyone," Nigel says. "Now rip those suckers up and throw the paper into the air."

Stephen's is folded into a paper jet that he launches around the room. Jill looks so pretty throwing hers, it makes Trixie say, "It's like a wedding." But Vanessa's paper is so small there is no ceremony to shredding it. Instead the pieces turn into torn-by-a-gerbil-sized balls that fall through her fingers onto the table. And worse, when the ritual is over, she still feels old. She scoops up the dirty little pieces of paper and crams them into her pocket.

"All right, each of you needs to keep the ritual going. Find the one that works best for you and commit to it. If necessary find a series of ritualistic steps to blow up your anxiety." Nigel looks directly at Vanessa as he says these last words. He locks eyes with her and continues, "But for now, more writing. Go forth and proliferate. That includes you too, Vanessa."

She stews in the chair at the back of the yard. She can't stand that not only is she blocked from writing, she's blocked from even having an effective ritual. She picks one of the small balls of ritual paper from her pocket and launches it across the yard with her forefinger. It lodges in the blackberry tangle. She hopes it's the piece with the word *old* written on it and that a Douglas squirrel will find it and bring it back to its nest where a litter of babies is being reared. *What's old becomes young again*, she thinks. She writes those words down and starts to think about the remains of the joint wrapped in the foil in her room. *A remnant from when I was young?* she wonders. Maybe it might help quell the panic she's feeling. There is only the afternoon and the next morning left for her to write something meaningful, and it looks like nothing is going to come together.

Vanessa flips to the page in her journal where she'd begun to write *Spring Breakup*. She runs the pen through the title and changes it to *Marriage Breakup*. A few new words creep onto the page.

Brilliant sunshine caught us under
the bell jar of our honeymoon,
anxiously examining all our nuptial parts.
Mandibles, shamefuls, wings and hearts.

So soon his sails unfurled, his rigging squared,
he flew across the lake,
while I waited back on sandy shore
a collector's pin in hand.

Frozen I remained, for time to come,
still every year it's a surprise when the ice goes out,
the fish floats up, a sign the seam has split—split at the seam.
The pin still firmly held in hand.

She looks at the poem. It's beginning to take shape, although she doesn't like the look of the uneven lines, and she changes the title back to *Spring Breakup*. After all it had been spring when she and Dick began to split. She remembers the day she moved into the den and made a cave for herself. The sun had been shining and the tulips were beginning to bloom outside the window. But what's with the pin in hand? She can feel it right now, a genome of ancestral experience tingling at a small spot on the end of her thumb and forefinger. Waiting to do something. But what?

THE COUPLES ARRIVE for lunch in a ball of pulsing energy. They're readying for their final night *rave* in the woods. Although Vanessa is jealous of their exhilaration—she's in line behind one couple who breathlessly make plans to collect feathers after lunch for headdresses—simultaneously, she's relieved she won't have to do anything so tribal. She's about to mention bird mites to the couple, when Joshua and Paula slide in front of her with the ease of entitlement that comes from being the leaders of the biggest tribe.

The two of them begin to enthusiastically go through a playlist for the evening's music. Vanessa overhears Hebrew wedding dance, Kenyan dance loop, First Nation's remix of *Good Ship Lollipop,* and Sly's *Family Affair.* At the mention of Sly, her mind drifts to the fringed couture halter-top she'd bought years ago in Yorkville and had thrown into her luggage at the last minute before coming away. Maybe she should put it on later, for the fun of it.

Lunch is polenta spears with Kalamata olives on romaine lettuce fresh from the Laurel Bush garden, together with as much wheat-free, green goddess dressing as Vanessa can scoop onto her plate. She loves the dressing and is gobbling it up when she decides even though she's not invited to the rave, she'll dress for a party later anyway. She can dance alone in the A-frame to the strains of music that will filter through the woods from the ample sound system she'd seen being dollied through the trees earlier that morning.

By contrast to thoughts of a rave, the afternoon workshop is dull. It ends with Nigel asking everyone to think about the one thing they will come away with, to record this thing in a ceremonial way, and to be ready to keep it in a place of prominence. He dismisses them for an hour to ponder this one thing and create an artifact that reflects it. The length of time surprises Vanessa. Nigel seems to want some deep thoughts on this issue, which only serves to freeze over her creative power. Or maybe he's just running out of steam, in which case she's pissed off.

When they reassemble, Trixie has made a small weaving with a finger loom that stitches out the words *I will pray*. Stephen has carved *Keep on Writing* into a block of wood. Julie, who also turns out to be a dancer, performs a short piece she calls *Juicy Artist* that she asks Barbara to video for her. The creepy guy who never talks has a blank piece of driftwood that he says will be his tablet of ever-changing creative visions. RainDear holds up a painting of a rainbow. Alicia has recorded a dissertation into Dragon-Maker, which Nigel asks her to turn off after the Dragon has finished reciting a beat poem: *crystal-ize-ize-ize the na-na-nadir/ celestial-celestial power to the ze-ze-ze-zenith/ crystal-ize-ize-ize the ze-ze-ze-zenith/ destroy-oy-oy the underbelly-belly-belly of the na-na-na-nadir.*

When Nigel gets to Vanessa, she picks up a small piece of fabric on which she has stitched the words *Find the Ritual* using the thread from her travel sewing kit. She expects Nigel will pass her by, but instead he begins to riff on what she's said.

"This is profound. It's the recognition of the power of the primordial which is the wellspring of creativity. Sleep on the ritual, Vanessa, and it will come to you. Bring it to the front of your mind and you will see it."

"I already feel it," she surprises herself by speaking.

"What do you mean?"

"I already feel something tingling in my fingers. I just don't know what it is."

"Honour those fingers. They will lead you to it. Thank the

power of the primordial for whatever it brings. It's the message you are meant to hear. Make a ceremony and you will discover the message."

THE STRINGS AT THE BACK of Vanessa's halter-top tangle after she makes a ceremony of smoking the rest of the joint. The tingling that has been in her finger and thumb all afternoon is so strong she can barely handle putting on the top. Once she's got it on properly, she digs into her clothing drawer to find the leather shorts she made years ago back in Victoria. She pulls them on and feels so full of excitement and energy, she begins to stamp out a dance in her room. The fringes on the halter jiggle throughout her body as she runs outside.

She has to slow down, this is too stimulating. She has not felt this charged in years, and decides she better head to the refuge of the Laurel Bush garden. As she pushes open the gate, she pulls out a seed head that somehow had got stuck in the slats. It looks like a small human face with exploding hair. She is sitting under the apple tree pondering it, when one of the gardeners walks in her direction.

"What is this?" she extends the head toward him.

"It's from an ornamental onion called *Allium Schubertii*. It's named after the composer."

"It looks like him."

"I guess. I don't know what he looks like."

"Like this."

"Really?" He laughs.

The gardener moves toward a pile of tubers that resemble little twisted human bodies. He begins to sort, discarding various fleshy ones that seem perfectly fine to her. She does not like to watch the discards pile up like corpses.

"What are these?" she asks.

"Dahlia tubers."

"Why are you throwing some of them away?"

"We have lots, some of these have a little mold on them."

She picks one of the freshest and biggest looking tubers from the discard pile and fits the stem of the Schubertii head into its neck.

"Look. He lives," she says.

"Schubert rocks." The gardener smiles.

Pleased with her creation, Vanessa stands to take in the life-affirming smell of the compost heaped behind the gardener. She looks over the gardenscape. She wonders how she'd missed the majestic blue delphinium at the end of the row looking out to the sea. And the lush bushes of cosmos, paper white and bubblegum pink, wavering delicately in the wind. She strolls the rows of kale, carrots, chard, and beets, and with her mind full of colour and life, she walks back toward the A-frame.

She places Schubertii on the pillow of her bed and goes outside to stand on the stoop of her door to listen for the dinner triangle. Its ring signals the start of a stream of couples—coupledom in costume—headed for the dining hall before their rave in the woods. In the first minute a man dressed as a Buddhist monk, his wife as a geisha, a couple in snorkel gear possibly portraying divers from *Life Aquatic with Steve Zissou*, and the bird-headdress pair all walk by. Vanessa feels hollowed out with a desire to participate in their ritual. At the bottom of her hollowness, she starts walking toward the nude artist's cottage.

Until she breaks through the canopy of foliage around his cabin, she believes she's mostly on this trek to buy more wine. But as soon as she sees him sitting naked at his easel, she knows it's his company she's seeking.

"Well look who it is," he says. "My friend the scaredy cat."

Vanessa comes around the deck to have a look at his painting. She recognizes the scene. "That's the beach in front of Laurel Bush, isn't it?"

"Yes, the sward."

"A sward? What's that?"

"It means a grassy place. I like this spot because it's at the ocean where there are remnants of an orchard. Kind of a metaphor for civilization meeting the wild."

"It's good," she says.

"Yep. This one is turning out okay. I think they'll take it at the gift shop. Have a seat," he gestures toward the empty cedar chair.

Vanessa doesn't protest. She watches while he makes a few more strokes, then cleans his brush.

"Excuse me," he says rising from his chair.

"Sure. I didn't mean to intrude."

"You're not."

When he returns, he's wearing pants and a green t-shirt with yellow lettering that says *Take It All Off.*

"You didn't have to dress for me," she says.

"I know, but it's good to be formal when I have a visitor. Or did you want to buy some more wine?"

"I thought I did, but now that I'm here I'm okay just visiting. What's your name by the way?"

"Finn."

"I'm Vanessa."

When Finn offers her tube steaks and potato chips for dinner, she doesn't protest. In fact, hot dogs roasted over the fire on sticks that Finn has sharpened with his penknife taste surprisingly delicious, especially after a week of all organic. As the sun begins to set, the two of them are comfortable burning coloured marshmallows on the ends of the sticks (all but the pink ones which

Finn has declared are spiked with red dye no. 4). Finn blows out a green marshmallow that he's caught on fire, and pops it into his mouth.

"Oh boy," he says. "Too hot." After he finishes munching it, he comes and stands behind Vanessa putting his hand very lightly on her bare back at the spot that would touch her heart if he were to drill through to the front of her chest. It makes her shoulders open like a dove's wings. For a second she thinks she'll pass out if her wings touch anything.

"You must be cold," he says as his hand spreads across her back.

It surprises her when he leaves to disappear inside his cabin again. He returns with another *Take It All Off* t-shirt. "You can keep it," he says, "I have a few. A friend gave them to me from a recycling campaign he worked on for the island."

"Thank you. A souvenir," she says.

She puts the shirt on and Finn says, "What's troubling you, honey?"

Vanessa doesn't know how to answer. Despite his youthful vigour, he is likely as old as she is, so she can't be rude and say, *I don't like being the age I am.* But then, she says it anyway.

"Ha. I'm sure I have you bested by a couple of years," he says. "It's not so bad."

"Okay, then I don't like being the age I am and alone. And coming on this retreat has made me believe I am not a nice person. I can't *celebrate* like the others."

"Celebrate. Hogwash. Sometimes it's just not the right time to celebrate. Not everything has to be pumped over the top."

"I know. But somewhere along the way I lost the ability to look inward and find any of the good stuff."

"I think it's in there. Don't be so hard on yourself. Then maybe you won't be so hard on others."

Vanessa shoves a pink marshmallow onto the end of her stick and holds it to the flame.

Finn laughs, "You don't have to commit suicide over this."

They sit together in silence for a time. Then she stands, and he does, too. They hug. She breathes him in. She breathes him out, and that's all that's required. Nothing pumped over the top. Nothing really to celebrate. It just is.

"Well, I should go," she finally says.

"Wait. I want to give you a real souvenir of your visit."

He disappears inside and comes out with a burlap bag. "It's a bit of a ritual I go through to see what people pull out. Tells me about their spirit side."

"That's funny, we're supposed to be working on ritual at the workshop."

"Well go ahead. Plunge in and find out who you are."

"Ow," Vanessa exclaims when something spears the end of her finger. It hits at the very spot that hasn't stopped tingling since morning. She pulls out what looks like a porcupine quill with a duck feather stuck to it.

"Ha. Two for one," Finn says.

"I think I'm meant to take the quill," she smiles.

"Okay. I found that on Vancouver Island in Strathcona Park. Porcupines are kind of rare around here. It suits you though. A bit prickly on the outside, but rare and radiant on the inside. Yes?"

"Yeah. And always prepared," Vanessa waives her little flashlight along the path in front of her as a gesture of farewell.

"Okay. Shine on, beauty," Finn says. "It's been a slice."

THE TRIANGLE WAKES Vanessa a half hour earlier than usual. The last morning wakeup is designed to give everyone time to clear their rooms before breakfast, but she's in no hurry to rise. She can still feel the pressure of Finn's hand on her back. She'd enjoyed the hardness of his middle finger pressing near her spine.

When she finally does rise, she uses her time to gather everything together from the A-frame and get it out to the car. She plops Schubertii with his wild onion hair and dahlia body onto the passenger seat, so she'll have company during the trek back to the airport.

After a final breakfast of organic eggs and cornbread, she heads to Cedar Hall for the wrap-up. Nigel, who is apparently out of steam altogether, has little to say. For his parting shot, he invites people to tell one another what they are grateful for and besides all the usual *grateful for the group*, *grateful for the wisdom of the leader*, there is one odd comment from Alicia who sidles up to Vanessa for a private word.

"I'm grateful for your coldness," Alicia whispers. "It helped stop what could have been a very emotional experience for me."

As Vanessa backs out of the parking lot, she uses only thoughts that serve her well. *Surely I heard wrong. What Alicia meant to say was 'thank goodness for your coolness.'* Big difference in such a small temperature change—cold to cool.

She follows the green arrows toward the ferry. The trip seems a lot faster on the way out than it had on the way in.

Once she's safely on the ferry, no scratches to her rental, she has a clear view of the Strait. Next to her is Donna and Sarah's blue minivan. Donna helps Sarah out of the van so she can get a better look at the scenery. Sarah moves awkwardly without her wheelchair and Megabyte sits anxiously in the back seat watching them move toward the ferry's rail. Donna has done something different with her hair, hers no longer matches Sarah's. Instead hers is pulled back into a headband adorned with small jewels that catch the sunlight, while Sarah's hangs straight. As the shoreline advances, there is an unmistakable love passing between them. Vanessa feels a twinge of compassion, or is it regret for a loss of something that won't quite coalesce?

She picks up Schubertii, whom she knows now is not Schubert, but rather some other musician. A bass player who travelled everywhere with his scent and a quiver of instruments. She extracts the porcupine quill from her wallet. Her hand trembles. She waits for it to settle, the sharp quill frozen in midair over the carcass, one end fitting neatly into the tingling spots on her forefinger and thumb. Instinctively, she moves her hand back. Then she sinks the quill into the flesh of the tuber, and sits. She is elated to have committed.

Enchanted Girl

Tall and tan and young and lovely
—Girl from Ipanema, Antonio Carlos Jobim

Fairies whirl around Vanessa's face and land on her shoulders while Astrud Gilberto's voice floats from the transistor radio propped on the hood of her father's Mustang. Afternoon sun filters into the garage catching the specks of dirt in the air from Vanessa sweeping up behind the garbage bins. For a second, her family's debris turns to golden fairy dust, just like in *Midsummer Night's Dream* that her grade ten class had studied that year at school.

She looks down at her arms. They're tanned, but barely. It's taken nearly the whole summer broiling in the backyard, slathered in a mixture of Johnson's baby oil and iodine, to achieve this meagre result. Not to mention the ordeal of listening to her mother's whine, *You're going to be more wrinkled than I am if you're not careful.*

Yet despite the slick of baby oil that sometimes catches in her hairline and a barely-there tan, she is lovely, isn't she? Hadn't that boy who drives the red Volkswagen bus by the tennis courts said so? Isn't *hey girl, lookin' fine* as close to *lovely* as it's going to get from a skateboarding dreamer boy? And so what if her girlfriends say the boy is only looking to pick up anybody who'll share the cost of a drive to California. She knows the way he watches her is different from the way he watches the others. He even knows her name, called her over to his bus once and said, "Vanessa you sure would look gooo-ood in a bikini on Ocean Beach."

When she'd asked around, the stories she'd heard were beyond exciting. He's at least seventeen, and he's two grades ahead of her, though her friend Linda had heard he dropped out before finals because he's moving back to San Francisco to live with his father, who is either an actor, or a plumber, or possibly both. Kitty had told her his name is Steve, and that Steve's a good kisser, but he's more like eighteen because they put him back a grade when he moved to Canada. She knows this from her older sister, Liz, who Kitty says is still *into him* even though he stopped talking to her the day after he left her neck covered in hickeys.

All of this is cool, except Vanessa doesn't like to remember how Kitty had reacted when she admitted to a crush on Steve. "You're an idiot if you fall for him, he's so out of your league even Liz couldn't hang on," she'd said. And for a moment Vanessa believed her, because she is a nerd. She likes to stay home and fool around with Simplicity patterns in the basement, design her own clothing even on her mother's old Singer. Anyway, Kitty's sister Liz is starting to grow a moustache and probably it's only her boobs Steve is interested in—though she doesn't like to think about him that way—still, it's part of the attraction, that he likes her better than all the others, especially when you put it together with the story Jane had told her about him playing guitar in a Bay area band that's going to be the next Doobie Brothers. "They're waiting to release their first album, and that's why he has to get back to California so quickly," Jane had said. It all makes sense to Vanessa.

When she walks, she's like a samba.

Vanessa swivels her hips around the broom while Astrud sings.

She presses the handle into her body thinking about Steve's tanned chest and arms. He's fuller than most of the boys at school, and her body responds in a curious lush way to the hard angle of the broom. It's a new feeling. Sort of scary, but thrilling at the same time. She pushes the broom forward, making the fairy dust swirl to the crown of her head. The future gleams in front of her like the polished point of an opal, and in that moment she turns from being a generic *any girl* to an *enchanted girl.*

An enchanted girl could put the broom down and walk out of the garage all the way to Haight-Ashbury, just like her cousin Marion had. She could reinvent herself any way she wants. Write dangerous music like Grace Slick, smoke black cigarettes like Joni Mitchell, design flowers around any Laura Ashley prairie dress. She could even suck off Jim Morrison, if she wanted to and he wasn't already four years dead, and she had any clue what that really means.

She pulls the broom back into herself and kisses it, opening her mouth a bit like she'd seen Julie Christie do in the movie *Darling.* Then impulsively, she sweeps the dirt into a corner behind the side door, and with a mix of fairy dust, dead rock stars, and a red Volkswagen bus in her head, she walks out of the garage, down the driveway and toward the tennis courts.

A block in, she realizes she isn't wearing a bra. She nearly turns back except her ribbed tube-top doesn't work with a bra. Besides, he would respect her. He wouldn't venture beneath her top the first time.

As she approaches the courts, she starts to wish she'd put on some lipstick, maybe some of that strawberry-flavoured gloss her mom had given for her birthday. She imagines him tasting it, licking his lips at the delight of it. But as she hangs at the baseline of the court watching the bus drive down the street toward her, all thoughts of what she is or is not wearing fly out of her head.

The bus stops at the edge of the field, where she stoops to pick a daisy from a clump growing there. She offers it to him as she steps up into the seat. The bus smells of marijuana and patchouli oil, a smell she knows from Kitty's house, from the time Liz had some of her wild friends over, and they'd sat in the backyard toking and getting goofy, until everybody passed out, and only she and Kitty were left to clean up before the parents came home.

Steve takes the daisy from her and puts it behind her ear. "There," he says, "just like a real California girl."

He pushes in the clutch and with a roar the bus heads toward the high school. He parks it in the lot behind the football field, and kills the engines as he turns to ask, "You from around here?"

The question surprises her. She thought he knew they went to the same school.

"I'm from Islington," she says.

"Where in hell's name is that?"

"Here," she says pointing down between her legs. As she's doing it, she realizes how stupid it looks.

"This," he says pointing to his own crotch, "is Etobicoke."

"You're right," she smiles. "It's just that my grandmother corrects me when I say Etobicoke. She thinks Islington sounds better. It's what they used to call this place." Vanessa rotates her finger around trying to bring in the strength and wisdom of old Islington to guide her through this first encounter with what she now realizes is a real man. Not a boy. Not like Greg Peacock who sat behind her in English and was hopelessly in love with her nerdy fashions and her strawberry lip-gloss.

"Do you always do what your granny says?" he asks, as he removes her top with one smooth motion of the hand.

"No," Vanessa giggles, even though she doesn't feel like laughing. He hadn't asked if it was okay—and the way he'd done it—like he was flicking a tea towel.

"I like the halter you wore for me," he says.

He moves in to kiss a nipple.

Part of her wants to protest, except the kissing feels good, in an unexpectedly *gooo-ood* way. Still she's uncomfortable, worried that one of the boys fooling around on the football field might see them. So she tries to push his head away, change the mood of their encounter.

"I hear you're going to San Francisco," she says. "Want some company?"

"Come on," he says, "you got me all worked up here."

His hand moves toward the drawstring on his jam shorts and soon he's exposed, urging her head down toward him.

She hasn't been down very long and doesn't even know what it is she's done to make the warm spurt of liquid that hits her cheek, but when it's over he seems happy enough. And no sooner has he cleaned up the puddle in his pubic hair, licking his fingers as he goes, than he's firing up the bus again and heading back toward the tennis courts.

When she descends from her seat, the daisy she'd given him falls to the pavement beside her foot. He drives over it with only a *see you* as he goes, and she watches his bumper with the neon peace sticker disappear, while she stands and thinks about how he hadn't even asked if she wanted a drive home. But maybe that's the way more experienced people do it. Besides it's no big deal sucking someone off. Next time he might take her up on her offer to drive to California with him. Or maybe she'll just go by herself. The possibilities are still endless, just not quite as gleaming as before.

HER MOTHER is waiting for her in the garage. The sun filtering through the open door is no longer golden, it's more of a burnt orange.

"You walked out of here," her mother says, "without putting the lid on the can and the dog threw garbage everywhere. Look. Behind the door. Look at the big pile of dirt you swept here. Do you see?"

But she doesn't see. She just doesn't see.

Because Vanessa is still the enchanted girl, although she does wonder how to live a life enchanted when the golden fairy dust has burned to orange.

Tremulous Treble

Jake wants Brian to leave his cabin so he can lie down. He puts his foot on the bed beside where Brian's tall frame sits hunched. He looks down at his lanky shoulders and asks, "Have you got your charts together for tonight?"

Brian squints up at him, "Course I do, man. Some of us want it so bad, we piss blood."

"So that's what I see in the toilet every morning." Jake doesn't make eye contact when he says this.

Brian lets out a sigh and sits up straight, as if he's just remembered there's no bunk bed above him. Having a stateroom of his own is one of the so-called perks Jake gets for being the musical director on the SS Prince Hawaiian.

Jake peers through the tiny pinhole that's supposed to be his sea view.

"Finally. We're coming into Kona," he says. "The lounge will be packed tonight. Maybe we'll get a little eye candy."

"With this crowd? Not a chance." Brian slaps the night table by the bed with the pent-up energy of a young man thwarted.

"You don't know. Some rich guy's hot wife might knock him out with a brandy and a hand job. Go on the prowl."

"Never, man. Just be glad this isn't the nudist cruise. Ugliest bunch of cretins I've seen in a long time."

"At least since the last cruise you were on. Yeah? Okay Mr. Brian the Bone Goodman. Outta here. Go limber up that trombone of yours. I got stuff to do."

Jake holds the door open for Brian and inhales the stench of the empty wine boxes stacked in the hall. When he took the job, he'd thought *own room* meant like a passenger, not some broom closet three levels down at the seasick end of the ship, right beside the kitchen garbage. It's the seventh week of his contract, and he's memorized the kitchen's routine by what's in the discard pile. Today is demi-glace day, gallons of cheap red wine boiled up with the bones left from the standing rib the night before. The hall stinks like a drunken dead man. A smell he's been familiar with since his father died.

He strips off his clothes to lie on the bed and stare at the ceiling. The truth is, even though the musicians have to pick Saran Wrap from the lounge chairs at the end of the evening, he likes the nudist cruises. He wishes he was on one now. This trip—the badly named Sunset Jazz Cruise (most of what they're asked to play isn't even jazz)—has set new levels of boredom. The passenger music appreciation level is calibrated by the amount of energy remaining in the collective of hearing aid batteries assembled in the room. And there's nothing like having a bass solo drowned in the buzz of a dying battery while somebody's wife shouts, *Take out your hearing aids, Fred.*

At least on the nudist cruise, the entertainment never ends. It's beyond bizarre watching naked people do everyday things like scope out the dinner buffet, play a game of shuffleboard, or learn to Watusi. Although even Jake has to admit too many jiggling bits on the dance floor is reason enough to take the *Limbo Song* and *The*

Twist from the set list.

Eventually he gets off the bed and walks the three short steps to his closet where he pulls jobbing suit number two from the rack. He wipes down the collar with a face cloth, removing what he can of the lint and dandruff, then carries the suit to the porthole to see what he's missed. The suit was new for the cruise, but the jacket is shiny already from where the bass rubs. He throws the jacket on the bed so he can survey the pants. They're almost threadbare from picking up his amp, moving it from room to room for the different gigs. Next time he signs on, if there is a next time, he's going to ask for a jobbing suit allowance. This is his shortest contract ever, but even at eight weeks the time at sea is taking a toll on more than just his suits. There's no chance for him to line up any kind of steady work for his own band. No chance even to find decent members for the band.

He's thirty years old, and he feels the pressure of time like a physical force on his back. No longer can he be the *enfant terrible* of the music world. The fact his career has taken up residence on a cruise ship might just mean he's a terrible musician, period.

BY THE TIME Jake gets to the lounge, Brian's already there, noodling into the mic, checking the sound levels. His croon works well for the lounge, and his dance man stuff is perfect for the weekly show. Brian's turned out to be a great hire even though Jake doesn't usually like trombone in a trio.

Skip, the drummer, is a different story. He arrives on the edge of being late and slides his stool in behind Jake. The metal leg catches the cuff of Jake's pant. They both hear the fabric tear.

"Damn," Skip says.

"Just another notch," Jake mumbles.

Skip tries hard, but there can be a lot of crashing going on when things are meant to be quiet, and he doesn't get that a good drummer is supposed to follow the bass player's solo. And for sure he doesn't get the pecking order of things, has no hesitation in cutting Jake's lawn, especially when it comes to the ladies. Not that Jake is into it like he used to be, or at least so he's pledged to Vanessa back home. Still, that contest over the ship's masseuse had left them bruised and pissed off with each other, despite both losing out in the end to the dining room manager.

Jake pulls a scratch of paper from his pocket. "Charts," he calls. "Okay in this order, *In a Sentimental Mood*, *Night in Tunisia*, *Salt Peanuts*, *Perdido*, *Body & Soul*, *The Lady's a Tramp* …"

"For the rich guy's hot wife?" Brian interrupts.

Jake steps back in mock indignation, "May I resume gentlemen?" He glances over at Skip, "And when she gets here, she's mine. You remember that, young fellow."

Skip flicks a brush on his snare, then uses it to salute, "Aye, aye captain. Sir!"

JAKE IS HOLDING THE SCRATCH that is the second set list, when Brian lets out a low wolf whistle—"She's here!" The three of them swivel to watch a statuesque all-American blonde wiggle her way across the lounge to take a seat at the bar.

Jake grabs his Fender and makes a hot thumb and a bit of a body hump before reading the chart list. When he's finished, Brian pipes up, "No *Voulez-Vous Coucher Avec Moi* this set?"

"Who said that wouldn't be happening?" Skip laughs.

Jake is aware the blonde is boring holes into his back while he plays through the set. Every time he bends to adjust his amp, he sneaks a look behind. She is unabashed.

Once the set is done, he heads to the bar to order a soda water. He wants something stiffer, but staff's not allowed to drink alcohol in the passenger lounge. The bartender, a friend, pushes his glass farther down the bar than is necessary, but Jake doesn't have to make a move. The blonde does it for him.

"What was that last number?" she asks, her lips pouting just enough.

He lowers the soda from his mouth, "It Don't Mean a Thing."

"If it ain't got that swing. Right? I like that. Though not everything has to mean something. Don't you agree?"

"Absolutely. A lot of things don't mean anything at all."

It turns out to be way too easy for Jake to sleep with her. She's gorgeous, she's into him, she's on the ship for just one night, to cruise to Maui (she knows somebody who knows somebody), and most importantly, he won't have to see her again on the decks and pretend to still be into her when he isn't. Except, as she's readying to leave the next morning, he is still into her. It hurts when he asks for her name and she says, "You don't need to know, Xavier. Call me Charo. This was fun, let's keep it that way."

When she clutches her handbag and wiggles her ass out the door, Jake follows. And as she disappears into the throng at disembarkation, he's left standing at the bottom of the gangplank waving to nobody.

Back in his cabin, he takes off his clothes to lie on the bed and puzzle over what had just happened. This is such a short contract, he'll be back home in Victoria before his body barely realizes he's left. So why had he done it? Even more, why does the thought of returning to Vanessa give him such a sinking feeling?

After a very short ponder, he begins to suspect it's that look. The look Vanessa has started to give him whenever he leaves the apartment, even if it's only to go around the corner to buy a quart of milk. A look of such deep disappointment, it bores to the centre of his core. Says he's a bad person. Makes him think, *Why do I even bother to try*?

He should be practiced at the look. After all, he's been seeing it for years going back to when he was a kid. The first time he can remember it, all he'd done was ask his mother if he could go on an overnight to Fredericton with his high school band mates. They'd been hired to play a gig. A real gig, with travel expenses and a hundred bucks from the door. And it wasn't like he'd been asking to go across the country. He remembers wheedling with her, "Fredericton isn't even two hours from Saint John. How can you stop me?" But a part of him knew that it was too soon, that he should have waited. She'd been sitting in amongst that jumble of half-finished afghans and quilts that forever seemed to be her life, her hand clasped around a can of beer. And she'd had that look of deep disappointment when she spoke and said, "If you go Jacob, you'll forever be my fallen angel."

But he owned one of the first Stooges' albums, Iggy Pop was his idol, and he was destined to become a great rocker too. So nothing, not even Lucifer himself, was going to get in his way. Still it nearly broke him when he walked out the front door, and his mother had come at him with one of her quilts, tried to put it around his shoulders. "You need it to keep warm," she'd said. "They should have covered your dad up. They shouldn't have let him lie in the cold like that. Please son. Cover up. Don't go like your dad."

His mother was the fallen angel.

Then there's that about Vanessa, too. Who knew when she'd told him that afternoon over tea at Murchie's that she was a fashion designer, what it really meant was she lives her life like his mother, surrounded by mismatched swatches of fabric and unfinished sewing projects. He'd thought fashion designer meant artist, not demented quilter. He needs the artist in her to come out, not the leader of the ladies' sewing circle. Not someone who spends time memorizing the names of famous bass players. Nor someone who tries to inhabit him by attempting to play that badly-tuned ukulele he'd left at the apartment. And oh god, the time she'd followed him into the band room at Harpo's, and sat in the corner plunking and singing with that awful tremulous treble of hers. She'd sounded worse than Tiny Tim. So dreadful, he'd had to ban her from coming to gigs with him.

These thoughts make Jake dizzy with sleep. Before he passes out on his bed, he flips through his fake book to be sure he's got everything he needs to appear prepared for the upcoming evening. Just one more week of this, he thinks, as he shoves the book under the covers.

FINAL NIGHT ON THE CRUISE is always a Club night, which means the full eight-piece band is there to politely contend with a lot of goofy requests and pretend to play their hearts out on numbers like *Celebrate*, *Shake Your Booty* and *Freak Out.* After the band plays *Y.M.C.A.* for the second time, the guy with the Indian headdress having finally shown up, Jake turns to Skip and says, "Okay, we're going to wrap up the musical end of things for this cruise with *Wipe Out.*"

Skip, whose forehead already has a slick on it like a big-old piece of deli meat left on the table too long, makes an audible groan. But he gamely picks up his sticks and plays enough of a surfer riff on the tom to send his band mates scrambling for the chart. When Jake feels a collective readiness, he counts, "One, and two, and you guys screw … uh, uh, uh." After a couple of notes, the spry old guys are out on the floor jumping like surf's up and they've got on new surfer jams. Most everybody who joins in looks as if they're about to break a hip. Still it's a good vibe, and a cheer goes up when Brian shouts, "Wipe Out!" and leaps from the stage onto the dance floor to begin an oddly-sexual dance that includes a full body shake every time Skip crashes a cymbal.

Jake likes ending the cruise this way. There's not a lot for the bass to do on this number, so he doesn't have to contend with the over-busy keyboardist who's playing attack bass with his foot anyway, and he gets to watch the band entertain.

When the number is finished, Jake turns to Skip and says, "Nice work with the high hat chick on two and four. You got it all going on tonight."

Skip looks pleased. Later, in the staff lounge, he asks Jake, "Can I spot you a drink? It's been good working with you."

Jake, who is already into his third beer and feeling some of the early fuzzy high of cruising into homeport, turns, "No, I insist. What can I get you?"

"Ginger ale."

"That's right. You don't drink. Good on you. You'd be a match for my girlfriend, Vanessa. She doesn't drink much either."

"You have a girlfriend?"

"Yeah. Kinda have to feel sorry for her, don't you?"

"Sort of. I mean, you know. Sorry."

"It's okay. I get it."

By the time Jake finishes his fourth beer, he's contemplating what it might be like to set Vanessa up with Skip. He's not sure whether it's the alcohol or having found a solution to his problem that makes him feel relieved, but when he's standing talking to Brian his head is in the mindset of a single man who has nothing on his brain but music.

"Tell me, Brian the Bone, why do some musicians piss blood?"

Brian leans back as if what he's about to say might smell bad, or cause Jake to do something physical. Instead, Brian is the one who makes a motion with his arm like he's throwing a football. "Cause they haven't been able to keep their art underneath their arm while they go rushing into the end zone," he says.

"They fumble?"

"No. The ones who piss blood are too good for that, but they've let a bunch of losers get in the way. You can't get into the zone with lightweights on your team."

Jake looks at Brian. "Maybe I'm the loser."

"You will be if you don't get off this cruise gig. You gotta form your own band, put a tour together. Me, I'm headed to Cuba next."

"For a kid, you're pretty smart."

"Street smart. Personally, I think your university music fucked you, man. That Mus.Bac. is only good for teaching high school and being the boss on a cruise ship. You lost your roots trying to play so many styles. My advice, just do one thing awesome."

Jake looks down at his feet and smiles. "I think I see a little Dee Dee Ramone sprouting from my big toe."

THEY FOUND JAKE'S father's body frozen to the floor in the bandshell at King's Square in Saint John. Nobody knew where he'd been earlier in the evening, or how long he'd been there, but probably most of the night, after he'd been kicked out of some pub or other. At first the authorities refused to bring him home, said the body had to go to the morgue and from there to a funeral home or burial. But Jake's mother had gone crazy on them. She screamed that it was her family's custom to have a viewing in the front parlour, and it was her right to do so, that she'd get a court order if necessary.

They brought his father's body back embalmed inside a closed casket and left it on the living room floor where it sat for a week like a beacon of doom. When they returned to get him the final time, his mother was so collapsed with fatigue and drink she no longer had the strength to argue with them.

Jake knew it didn't make sense that he could smell his father inside the casket, but he swore he could. The musty fermented stink of death by alcohol permeated his nostrils long after the casket was removed. He could still smell it months later when he'd asked to go to Fredericton. It wasn't right to be seventeen years old and spend all your time with your mother. And just like the stench of his dead father remained, so did that look of deep disappointment in his mother's eyes.

WHILE JAKE STANDS at the closed door to the apartment in Victoria on Pandora Street, before he even knocks, he can see the look in Vanessa's eyes. He feels like a bee trapped inside a mason jar, banging up against the walls of his history. He inhales a big breath and raps on the door. As she opens it, he knows whatever is about to come out of his mouth will be wrong. It will hurt. He will fail.

"Hey, Vanessa."

"Hey, Jake. You're back. Nice to see you."

"You too. How's things?"

It all feels so awkward. After she blurts, "I had an abortion," the field in front of him is suddenly littered with fallen angels. He makes an involuntary grip of his arm muscle, like somebody might steal the art right out from under him, and he wants to cry because he is becoming his father, and that can't happen or he will die frozen to the sidewalk full of trampled dreams just like his dad, so instead of letting himself go there, he makes a mumble of it, "Oh jeez. Thanks for handling that. Must have been rough on your own."

Then she is talking, a lot of words, he can see her mouth moving, but most of it he can't hear because the cycle of family is backed up into his head.

After a time, when the roaring in his head starts to clear, he does hear her say, "It's okay. You're right, I handled it. It feels good to be able to tell someone, though." And then, because he needs to believe that she is okay with it so he can keep on standing in the room and not bolt out the door and run all the way back to Saint John to beg his mother for forgiveness, which he knows, if he does, will mean he never plays another note of music again, and he'll get so sucked back into the never-ending black hole that is his mother's life, it will become his black hole again too, and because he so desperately needs for this not to happen, he just keeps on standing exactly in the same position until a part of him really does believe Vanessa has handled it, that she really is okay with it, despite him not being clear on what procreation that ends in an abortion even entails, all of it too huge and godlike for him to consider, so to take it out of this place of fallen angels and into the church of his art, he hears himself say, "Do you want to come see a band at Harpo's with me tonight?" He says this despite knowing he's on his way to the club with the hope that something meaner and tougher will be there waiting for him.

He holds his breath, hoping against hope Vanessa will say no. But fallen angels never do as they are asked. As she walks closer to the door, readying to leave with him, pulling on the cherry-coloured jacket she made herself, the one with too much padding in the shoulders, Jake feels a sudden unscrewing of the lid on the mason jar, a pop of the hermetic seal around the relationship. She moves forward for a kiss, but he is already hurtling down the field toward the end zone leaping over fallen bodies that aren't able to see who it is that's flying above them. He pushes out the door ahead of her, and her lumpy shoulders, because there's barely any time left.

Killer Bass Line

It happened during her third month at Amadea, the design shop she was lucky enough to land a job with in Victoria. It was the only good shop in the city at the time, unless you counted the tailor in Oak Bay who wore half-glasses at the end of his nose and mostly produced heavy tweed fashions for seniors. It was 1985, and she was fresh out of the George Brown fashion program and incredibly happy to have made it to the West Coast—the place, her father liked to joke, where everything loose eventually rolled because the world is on a westward tilt.

Her parents were disappointed she'd even gone into fashion after completing a degree at the university. What can you do with a fashion diploma? her mother had asked. All the way to Victoria, her father had said. But the truth was, almost the minute Vanessa stepped off the plane, thoughts of returning to Toronto left her head.

She loved everything about Victoria. The fields strewn with pumpkins on the drive from the airport, the sparkling water in the inner harbour, the exotic tiny Chinatown that was also her new neighbourhood, her boss, Amadea, her co-workers, Myra and Gary, the logger named Rob that she liked to get high with, and the cute fisherman named Grant who was so much fun it didn't matter if he had a girlfriend in every cove up the coast.

Then, in that third month, she met Jake. The bass player she consciously tried to build borders around, tried to fend off in her mind, but never could in her body. She knew his ego was outsized and he had bad personal habits. But the thing she couldn't work around was the way he took her to bed. She wondered if it had something to do with his ability to snuggle into the bass like it was the most precious thing in the world.

They met in an incense shop in Fan Tan Alley—their hands glancing off one another as they both reached for the same package of pine incense.

"What do you need incense for?" he asked.

"To mask the smell of the kitty litter," she said.

"Well, as long as you don't keep the litter in the bedroom, I'm there."

They barely finished their mugs of tea at Murchie's before she was leading him up the stairs to her flat above the vintage clothing shop on Pandora Street, where she introduced him to her cat Shadow and her dress dummies, and they spent the next forty-eight hours tangled in a love-lock. It was the sweetest time Vanessa could remember. He brought her tea in the evening when she was chilled, and cold watermelon in the heat of the afternoon. All the while she kept telling herself *be careful, be careful, don't fall for this one.* Despite the self-warnings, she let him take the next six months to move in.

The way he explained it, "I don't really have a home base. I work here, Vancouver, Seattle, Portland—wherever Roger Waters, Dee Dee Ramone or Charlie Haden isn't—so I might as well make this home."

And see him she did, because he hardly ever wore clothing when they were alone in the flat. "I like to feel the bass on my tummy," he said. At first, she thought it was funny, especially when it was cold and his balls shrank up. But soon she started to nag about it, tried to push him off the couch, make him sit on newspapers, particularly when he needed a bath and he sat on their pale pink couch. Then after a time it wasn't worth the struggle, or the cold shoulder she got when she criticized. Besides, the truth was she was addicted to the smell of him, even when he was in need of a clean. So ultimately, she learned that to live with him peacefully was to put up with some exhibitionist bullshit and just let it be.

She never believed he was going to be as famous as the bass players he liked to pretend he was, but a lot of musicians were calling, some of them with names like Grease, Shrew and Huge. So he obviously had work, even if too much of it was on cruises that took him away for weeks at a time, and after which he always brought back more stuff—Mexican maracas, Hawaiian ukuleles, and a strange Alaskan instrument made out of caribou hide and a rusty hand saw.

She cleared the sewing supplies from the second bedroom, so he could make a music room, but in the end the entire flat was one big music mess. Scores, bows, cakes of rosin, keyboards, amplifiers—junk strewn everywhere. He said he knew who he was, and she should step around his things, be grateful for the flirtation he let her have with the musical imagination. The time he came back from Catalina Island and presented her with a pretty turquoise scarf, he'd gone down on one knee and said, "The colour and pieces of space in the music, all of this I give to you." Afterward, they'd had hand-over-the-mouth-screaming sex, and she was mad at herself for getting hooked back in.

Then there were the actual basses themselves. Jake had what he liked to call a *quiver*—six in all. At first he'd had them stashed in various cities at friends' homes, but every time he went on tour he brought back another one. First to come was the expensive Italian acoustic. He played that one at high-class supper clubs, and carried a bow with it to use on the last note of the ballads. He kept it in a case that seemed to double its size when, in his mind, it was out of the way. Next was the rough standup, with scratches all over the body and strings high off the fingerboard, that he thumped away at in the rockabilly bands. Then the traditional fretted electric that he took on the cruises, followed by the avant-garde bass that looked more like a whale's rib mounted on a peg. The rib's sound was lousy, but its appearance was right for the crowd that liked train wreck music. It didn't matter if its sound was no good, because those concerts usually had more members in the band than in the audience.

Then there was the bass that Vanessa loved. The fretless electric, a beautiful aquamarine instrument that Jake always put clothes on to play. "Takes the electric bass right out of being the bastard child of the acoustic," he said. But the mistake she made around that one was in trying to compliment him on its sound. She'd worked hard to learn everything she could about music and was proud that she was beginning to distinguish one musician from another.

"You sound like that guy in Weather Report," she said.

Jake set the aqua instrument down. "Are you crazy? Jaco is great, but my style is my own. I'm more punk." Then he took a dramatic pause, as if recovering from a terrible shock, and picked the bass back up, loosened a string, stuck a pick in it, and made a mean sound.

She couldn't help but laugh. He looked hilarious in the punk pose. But she was confused when she found the album with Jaco's famous song *Havona* hidden under a stack of tea towels in the linen cupboard. It was as if he didn't want people to know he even owned the record.

And finally there was the bass Vanessa hated. It was a knockoff Fender that Jake played in the punk bands who called way more often than she liked. He got in an ugly mood every time he played a punk gig. Once, in preparation for a *wild* night, he'd swung the bass around in the kitchen so violently, he broke the creamer to the Willow Pattern tea set she'd brought from Toronto.

"My grandmother gave me that," she wailed.

"Sorry babe, that's the price you gotta pay. I need to be in a thrash mood to do this gig with Art. The mighty man does not call often."

Ever after she hated the faux Fender. Hated the people he played it with. Hated the way he left it propped up in the spare room, looking like the dark lord of destruction glowering in the corner. She tried to put one of her dress dummies in front of it, but Jake slung the guitar around the dummy's neck and anchored her to the wall. "So you can think of me when I'm gone," he said.

MYRA AT WORK thought Jake was a jerk. "You should pay attention to the subtle stuff." Vanessa had been standing captive in the middle of the coffee table at the back of the shop, while Myra pinned up the hem of a tulle dress they'd designed together. The dress was for a wealthy patron, a young woman who'd married an older titan of industry but still fancied herself a bohemian. To make the point to the husband's *tweed crowd*, the woman had asked the shop to inset strips of doeskin into the bustier bodice.

"Like what subtle stuff?" Vanessa asked.

"Well I hate all that crap he's always saying—*I'm an artist. I need to be free.* Get away." Myra looked up at Vanessa, her mouth full of pins.

"Ew," Gary chimed in from the corner. "Get away. I agree"

"How would you know, Gary?" Vanessa turned to look at him.

"I date guys too, or did you forget? I know an asshole when I see one."

"You do indeed, my friend," Myra laughed.

"How can you talk with your mouth full of pins, Myra?" Gary ribbed.

"Years of practice."

Gary threw a piece of tulle at her.

MOSTLY VANESSA put on a brave face about the whole *needing to be free* thing, but after the first year, the truth was that it was beginning to get to her how much he was away. And even when he was in town, he had a million excuses for why she couldn't come to the shows with him. "The band rooms are stinky. Full of empty beer bottles. Club owners don't want girlfriends hanging around. The guys get uptight when they know people in the audience." The list was endless.

But the thing that really started to hurt was the matter-of-fact delivery of his mantra. "I need space. Period." He always made a little circle with his forefinger when he said the word *period.* One time, he even tried to intellectualize it into something that was supposed to be a positive. "The notes need space. To do that, I need space. I know the beats are there when I leave a space, just like I know you're there even when there's space between us. It's a type of respect I'm showing you, babe."

She so much didn't feel the respect, she didn't know how to put it into words. All she could manage was, "I can't take you seriously. Put on some clothes."

"Yeah. Yeah. I'm just getting dressed. I'm playing with the Lime Rickeys tonight over at Harpo's."

After he was gone, she sat on the couch with a sketchpad in her hand. She'd been working on some designs in her head that she wanted to sketch, but she couldn't draw. Her fingers felt cramped. She didn't like how love had shipwrecked her. Everything had been going along fine until she met Jake. Then she fell, and all of a sudden life was hard, and she was alone.

Alone. Alone. Alone.

A mind-numbing word if repeated too often. A word she couldn't get out of her head when she tried to fall asleep at night. Tried not to need him, her stomach twisted into a knot, making her sick. For three nights she went to bed like this. On the third night, her stomach felt so strange she started to wonder if she had cancer. When he came home later, smelling strongly of booze, and crawled into bed, he didn't even notice she was still awake.

Next morning he didn't hear her in the bathroom throwing up, was still lying on his back gently snoring when she left for the day. By the time she got home from work, he was gone again on yet another cruise. She knew he was going, but his note was too plain, simply said, "Back on the 27th possibly later." There was no hand drawn heart at the bottom, no *miss you* scrawled by his name, just the bare facts and not even that. The 27th of what month? It was the 2nd day of July, with any luck he'd be back at the end of August, but maybe not until September.

All that first week he was away, she couldn't eat anything but melba toast and stoned wheat thins. And every time she went into the bathroom at the shop to throw up, she'd had to turn up the radio. She thought she was hiding it, until Myra, her mouth full of pins again, looked up and said, "You're pregnant. Your bra size is bigger and you're throwing up all the time."

"I'm on the pill. I can't be pregnant. Besides, he's hardly around enough to get me pregnant."

"When was your last period?"

"No idea."

"Get a home test. First Blush is good. Two tests for the price of one, in case you goof the first try."

Vanessa wondered what Myra meant by *goof the first try* until she tried to pee into the tiny test tube that came with the kit. The tube was made for someone with a trickle no bigger than the outpouring of a parched mouse. Then on top of it there was the whole routine of setting the tube in the miniature rack, and waiting thirty minutes, without touching it, to see whether the ring at the bottom was blue.

And blue it was. No doubt about it.

When the results were official, the doctor said, "I hope it's what you want."

"No, it's not," she answered.

The doctor opened his hands and said, "You can't wait long if you want to do something about it. You're already into the third month." He presented it as an option with no consequences, but available for only a limited time.

That night she refilled Shadow's water dish so often it overflowed and made a puddle in the centre of the kitchen linoleum. Vanessa stepped in the puddle without feeling the water and walked over a newly penned score that Jake had left lying on the living room floor. The notes turned into a soft blur like an abstract Japanese watercolour, and when she finally noticed what she'd done, she stooped to pick up the score and read the word he'd written in the corner. *Leitmotif.* A word she knew meant a musical phrase that haunts, one that comes back on itself, again and again. "On its second or third hearing the phrase begins to remind you of itself," Jake had told her, "so it's never really finished."

She began to wonder if she was living with a second or third unfinished version of him. Or was she the one who was unfinished?

VANESSA DIDN'T TELL anybody about the results. At night a

new word crept into her head.

Abortion.

The word has to be repeated only once with intent to have the effect of an emotional lobotomy. By the time she returned to the doctor, she was so practised at feeling numb, it was easy to say what she needed.

"Have you thought this through?" the doctor asked.

"Yes," she lied.

"There's no going back," he said.

"I know."

GENERAL DAY SURGERY was a very busy place. Patients were lined up all around the waiting room, some with limbs in casts, some with only socks on their feet, some with open wounds barely contained, and a few, like Vanessa, who were apparently healthy.

"Do you have a ride home afterward?" the receptionist asked.

"Yes," she lied.

In pre-op, the pretty nurse who was covered to the eyeballs with a surgical mask, leaned in to ask, "Are you okay?"

"Oh, yes," she cried. The nurse held Vanessa's hand until she went under.

AFTERWARD she threw up in the taxi. She asked to get out a few streets before hers, so the driver could get to a clean-up station and she could breathe fresh air.

The Chinese grocer at the corner had cantaloupe melons on sale for 99 cents a pound. Most of the melons were overripe, and the small ones looked like babies' heads with the soft spots pushed in. It made her woozy to see them. At the empty flat, she crawled into bed and lay there like a wounded animal amidst Kleenex shreds and dog-eared magazines. She woke in the morning to the sound of a quiet boy's voice in her head. "Why did you do it, Mom?" he asked. She tried to answer. Tried to catch a glimpse of him before she was fully awake, but all that was left was a vision of curly golden hair and dark brown eyes, a lot like his father, and a bright light around his head.

On the way to work that morning, at the Chinese grocer's, the stack of melons had been replaced with fresh ones, and the price had gone up a dollar a pound.

VANESSA THOUGHT that when she told Jake, he might be angry she hadn't waited. Dishonoured somehow that she hadn't talked to him about it. Possibly even slightly disappointed things had been terminated. What she hadn't prepared for was for him to be so uncaring, in the pure sense of not caring one way or another.

"Thanks for handling that, babe," he said. "Must have been a bit rough I wasn't around." Then maybe because he did feel a little sorry, he asked if she wanted to come to Harpo's that night to see a new band from Montreal. "Start of a new thing in music. Quite a buzz about them. Sort of punk, sort of not. Got a chick on bass."

Vanessa didn't like the sound of it, but didn't think she wanted him to go alone. When she saw the goddess on bass, she was horrified she'd ever thought it could in any way have been okay for her to have come. The voluptuous blonde was playing a knockoff Fender, and Jake was behaving like the most inappropriate, lovesick groupie she'd ever heard him describe. He was hanging at the edge of the stage by the goddess, catcalling, or rather calling attention to himself, every chance he got. When the band finished its set, he mumbled, "Going to the band room."

He hadn't exactly told Vanessa not to follow him, though she knew she wasn't supposed to. By the time she got to the back hall, the room was already crowded, full of smoke and the sound of beer cans being opened. Jake pretty much filled the door in front of her, but she was able to see him reach over to shake the lead guitarist's hand, then not so much see as hear him turn to the goddess and say, "Killer bass line on that last number."

Vanessa saw a stiletto heel move off a chair, then open-legged fishnet stockings swivel full on around to Jake and say, "Well, aren't you the cutie."

That's when Vanessa watched their romance hit the beer-stained wall at the back of the band room just above the Echo and the Bunnymen poster. It was all she could do to stop herself from shouting into the cacophony, "I'm so inappropriate for him, even I can see it."

Then somehow in that moment it became mandatory for her to walk away. Not talk. Not look. Not think. Just walk.

Hunting Season

Dick has been by again. She can tell by the plop of salsa on the flagstone path. He always leaves something behind, an elbow smudge on the sliding door, a hand smear on the garden table, a fingerprint on the patio dimmer switch. He can't help it if his body gives off so much heat it leaves traces everywhere, but why would he bring a burrito, or calzone, or whatever overstuffed fast-food thing it was he'd been munching on, to her patio? Not having to clean up after someone else is supposed to be one of the perks of living on your own.

It's been almost two years since Vanessa bought Dick out of their house in Leaside, yet still he behaves like a confused dog that keeps returning to its spot on the porch. Surely he doesn't want to revisit the incident when she'd nearly clobbered him with the meat-tenderizing hammer. But he'd never worn a hat before in the city, not even on the coldest day. So why had he worn one that first time he came back uninvited? Had he believed the hat made him invisible? And why, when he'd asked if she'd thought about calling the police instead of almost bludgeoning him, hadn't she just told him the truth—*because somehow I knew it was you but you looked so stupid in that hat.* And then his excuse for being there—*because I miss the evening light and I just wanted to sit in the yard one more time*—all that had done was make her feel like a mean, old shrew.

It altogether feels unfair. Especially when she'd tried so hard to save the marriage in that first year after their beloved spaniel Lucy had died. One way or another, Lucy's dying had been the last straw. It was like the emotional bridge between them collapsed, and Vanessa simply got too worn down with the greasy fingerprints, the snoring, the cache of man stuff in the basement, and sadly, Dick's deescalating ego in most things. In the end, she'd simply needed to save herself from going under in a sea of toilet splatter and heaped towels beside the tub.

But the real kicker is that Dick only moved up the street from their house, to the Garden Court apartments, and he never even told her he was renting the corner suite, the one where she knew he could watch from his living room window whenever her car drove by, to say nothing about him knowing her favourite walking route through the courtyard was right beneath his bedroom window.

This is what really upsets her the most. Especially when she still has delusions she might meet a man and bring him home through the courtyard after pizza at Vero's. Maybe let the man stay the weekend if he's so inclined, even though it's never going to happen that she will eat pizza with a man at Vero's. Because the only people she ever meets are women, more women, and the odd man in a writing workshop who puts new meaning into the word odd. She only gets to observe men now—sitting at Starbucks staring hungover into the dregs of an Americano, shuffling the aisles of Valu-Mart searching for bargains—all of them looking like they could have given themselves a better shave or worn a decent pair of shoes.

At this point, she is prepared for Dick to come by now and again, secretly sometimes she even likes knowing he's been around. It's just that she wishes he hadn't chosen today of all days to do it. His presence has sullied the ground of her creative nest, all but physically pricked the pity sanctuary she's been working on since she received the email earlier in the day from the obscure little journal, *The New Orillian.*

The promise of her first publication should have been a thrill. And it was for a second, but too quickly it had put her into a depression about the lateness of it all, the confirmation that she could have been a contender if only she'd gotten down to it sooner. If only she'd started writing before she was so long in the tooth. It's too late now for her to be the wunderkind of any publishing house, not even a little-known house noted for its difficult, edgy works.

Just the same, the acceptance of her poem *Spring Breakup*, the poem she'd honed into an extended metaphor mapping the dissolution of her marriage, had boosted the creative forces that whirl in her head enough for her pick up a pen and spill out a few new lines:

some museum works of art remind of you
surrounded by hospital whiteness
standing alone from all the rest
sad and sometimes sickening
sick in colour
sad in spirit
great works of art nonetheless

These lines have nothing to do with Dick. And she doesn't want him anywhere near them. Yet she's kicking herself because she knows in a way it's her fault that Dick has come by. Getting started on a poem she's been mulling over in her head for half a lifetime had been exhausting, so too soon into it, she'd headed up to

Bayview for a cappuccino. But she shouldn't have cut through the Garden courtyard. And she shouldn't have gone around under Dick's bedroom window to sneak a peek at the last of the season's red begonias. She knew she was tempting fate, but she needed to figure out the essence of her poem, and to do that she'd impulsively decided she had to drink in a little of the begonia's blood red. Afterward, when she'd looked up to the golden maple growing in the centre of the courtyard, it had fused a feeling to the front of her brain. That feeling, she's sure, kicked off the rest of the afternoon's events.

She'd gone up to Starbuck's and waited in line to order her cappuccino. While she'd waited, she'd watched the clerks so busy flirting they couldn't get the customers' drinks out in any kind of timely way, and she'd pondered why it was that women always fall for the bad ones. She'd briefly thought about warning the plump barista with the purple hair that the too-thin, over-attractive guy wasting her time behind the counter was merely entertaining himself through his shift. That he had no intention of ever getting back to her seriously. But when the two of them eventually produced a cup of milky, separated cappuccino, she'd let it go, only mouthed the words *thank you*, and hit the sidewalk to catch the afternoon sun.

That's when she'd seen the boy. He'd come running straight at her, sun bouncing off his golden curls, a shining red halo behind him. The brightness had obscured his face and for just a moment he could have been any boy, anybody's boy. Her boy. The same boy who had come running after her in the dream so many years before, had asked her, *why did you do it, Mom?* So strange to hear your child speak only once, and then only in a dream after you had literally shattered him.

She'd stumbled at the sharp pain of her memory and banged into the young mother standing beside the boy. "Forgive me," she'd said.

"No problem," the young woman had answered.

Vanessa very nearly clarified. Almost said, "Not you. I'm sorry to the boy." But she'd pulled it together and kept moving. As she'd walked, another line came to her—*forgive me the glass womb you were consigned*—she'd stopped to scribble it down on the back of her Starbucks' receipt. It was a good line, although as she wrote it, she'd wondered whether she could use it. Had she made it up, or had she just heard it or read it somewhere else? This was so often the case with her in writing. All the good lines felt like they belonged to someone else. But she at least knew then that the poem she was writing was not in any way about the boy's father. It was about the boy himself.

After that, she'd taken the long way home, avoiding the courtyard, and for the rest of the walk golden boys were all she could see. In strollers, in the arms of happy mothers, running free in the park.

So this is the mood she's in when she spots the salsa on the flagstone path. She is sitting at the patio table in a semi-stunned space, staring down at the path, when she hears the sound of the latch on the side yard gate. Knowing that Dick has already been by, he should be the last person she expects to see, but she knows it's him before she turns.

"It's such a warm day for fall, Dick. Why are you wearing a hat again?" she asks.

"I take it you don't like the hat."

"Not especially."

Dick stands beside her and looks at the plop of red by her foot. "Sorry," he mumbles. "I'll clean that off."

He uncoils the hose on the side wall and begins to spray cold water at the salsa, some of it splashing up at Vanessa's ankles. After he's rewound the hose, he sits with her.

"Came by to get my duck hunting equipment," he says. "You weren't here before."

She says nothing. She'd known when she agreed he could keep his equipment in the basement, it would mean the duck hunting mess would never leave. Now that he's here looking for it again, she wishes she'd insisted it be gone.

"Do you mind if I go inside to get it?" he asks.

"Seems too early in the year for hunting," she says.

"First day of the season. Tomorrow."

"Really?"

"So?"

"So? What?"

"Do you mind?"

"Mind what?"

"Hey, what's eating you Vanessa? You seem very distracted."

"I am."

The two of them sit for a time. This is the same place they have been to many times in conversations over the years of their marriage. A place where one or both of them starts out on a specific quest for information or understanding, and the other simply drifts into a knot of misunderstanding, miscuing, or sometimes simply miss-caring. Then both of them get lost in the woods of emotion, and neither bothers to look for the breadcrumbs to find a way out.

In a moment of needing to get going, or perhaps simply of cooling down because the sun is finally starting to set, Dick asks again in a more personal way, "What's wrong? You seem unhappy."

"I am. There's someone I'm thinking about. Someone who I've thought about a lot over the years. But not for a while. Someone I need to say I'm sorry to, but can't."

Dick sits up straighter in his chair and scratches at his temple.

The motion adjusts his hat a touch, and Vanessa can see a corner of white underneath. White that looks like a bandage. She decides to say nothing, but wonders if maybe Dick got in a fight. That seems so uncharacteristic, but what else could have happened to his head?

"I guess that person is not someone you want to talk about," Dick says.

"Maybe I should. I never told you."

She watches as Dick's hand goes toward his head again as if to itch, but he thinks the better of it and lets the hand settle in his lap. She knows he probably thinks she's about to tell him something about another man, and she isn't sure how to start, so she starts with the other man.

"Well you know about that fellow Jake in Victoria. The one who was the bass player."

"Yeah. The guy the world was going to hear about, but never did. I know about that guy."

"What I didn't tell you is that I got pregnant with him."

"Oh. You have a child somewhere?" It seems to Vanessa that Dick is smiling a little. She's pretty sure the notion of a child somewhere is appealing to him. This adds a layer of confusion she had not contemplated.

"No. Sometimes I wish I did. But I terminated the baby. This is a very hard word for me to say. Baby. I haven't told very many people, including myself really. I don't usually think of him as a baby, in my head he's mostly just an it, and for a long time I didn't know whether I missed it simply because I wanted to be like everyone else and have an it. You know me, need to keep up with the neighbours. But I had a dream once when he came and spoke to me. So I know he's not an it. I've known for years, but for some reason I am, today, totally confused about him again. Today I feel like I need to say I'm sorry. But there's no one to say the words to.

And that makes me sad."

She stops. She knows, and probably Dick does too, that other than readings at her writing workshops, this is the most number of words she has said to anyone in at least five years. In the quiet of the moment, she realizes how little emotion she usually lets herself feel and that whatever amount she does have, she's been parsing out like there's a limited supply.

"You can say sorry to me," Dick says, "and I can try to use my energy with you to pass the message on to the boy."

Vanessa sits back in her chair. She realizes there is little chance anyone could have said it better than Dick, starting with, *The guy the world was going to hear about, but never did.* But she's afraid she might start to cry if she speaks right now. She looks up at the early evening sky instead. Trails of gathering darkness shimmer like delicate pulses. The whole sky looks organic, like a baby's veined hand struggling in the cocoon of night.

The two of them could have remained in silence for quite some time except that the next-door neighbour begins to fuss with his garbage bins. Then he decides this is the time to bring out his leaf blower and tease out the autumn detritus that has caught along the edge of the fence.

"What did the boy say?" Dick asks, raising his voice enough to be heard.

"He asked me, why had I done it?"

"And?"

"I didn't have an answer for him. I had nothing to say. For a while, I was so messed up, I even contemplated joining a nunnery. That is, until I really looked into it. No way. I couldn't take four prayers a night. Besides, it wouldn't have fixed anything. Still, I've never shaken the feeling there's something I need to make amends for."

"You know, none of this changes the way I think about you."

"Thank you, Dick. Some people would think the worse of me."

"Nothing to thank. Just the way it is."

"I've been thinking, though." Vanessa has to raise her voice to be heard over the advancing leaf blower, and Dick rubs his forehead, which cocks his hat even further back, as if to say, *What next?*

"I've been thinking that maybe I should have a burial for the baby."

Dick doesn't say anything.

"It would make me feel better," she says.

The neighbour turns off the leaf blower and Vanessa says *better* in too loud a voice.

"Okay," Dick says softly.

At this, she turns to look at him straight on and grabs his arm, "What happened to your head?"

"This," he says adjusting his hat. "It's nothing. A bit of work I had done."

"A bit. It seems like a lot."

What she can see of Dick's mostly bald head is crisscrossed with fine black stitches. One wound toward the front is seeping and it's that one which has the white bandage over it.

"The round last year, they went a little too gentle on me. They had to go deeper this time. But it's nothing, really. They got it all."

Vanessa is surprised how much this upsets her. How on the edge she feels with so many of her emotions. Invincible Dick has been cut. As she looks at him, there's a thought at the front of her mind that she can't say. *Nice guys like you take a lifetime to appreciate,* she is thinking. But she doesn't believe she has earned the right to say it yet. And she isn't sure what it would really mean if she did. Still, she appreciates the impish grin he's giving her.

Perhaps it's the length of the silence between them that compels Dick to go back a topic or two in their conversation.

"You know what they say about the first day of hunting season?"

"No. What?"

"They say, it's the day you settle your scores. Could be you need to do a little settling, lady."

"Okay. But first you tell me something. Why are you still here?"

"Maybe I'm just supposed to be here to watch what happens. Watch the relationship."

"Come inside," she says rising from her chair. "You can get your hunting equipment. And I need to get something upstairs."

While Dick is in the basement, Vanessa is in her bedroom searching the drawers of her bureau. She is looking for the dahlia tuber that's like a tiny human with an *Allium Schubertii* head—the dried ornamental onion flower that's like a head of explosive golden hair. When she finds it, she removes the porcupine quill that she'd plunged into the side of the tuber when she'd believed it was nothing more than a voodoo of Jake, the father of the golden boy. She feels real pain as she withdraws the quill and understands even more deeply the connection between her body and the body of the baby she'd shattered. She picks up the paper with the line of poetry on it that she's been keeping in the drawer beside the tuber. *The moon hangs like a bruised plum in the sky/ how dare he do this to me.* The line is about Jake and somehow it belongs with the body of their baby. She wraps the tuber in the paper, then walks across the hall into the bathroom. Under the harsh, fluorescent makeup light, she snips a piece of hair with her nail scissors.

When she joins Dick in the yard, he already has the shovel, the same one they'd used when they buried Lucy under the plum tree. She holds the tiny dahlia body in her hand and together they walk toward the tree. Dick clears away some fallen leaves on the other side around from where Lucy is resting. He hands her the shovel to dig. Vanessa thinks to herself, only with Dick could I have come to this place. This at least is something. Somewhere in this, there might be a joinder of sorts. She digs one layer deeper than she really needs to, before she lays the body draped in poetry into the little grave. She knows the words on the paper are not really accurate, but at least they evoke some essence of the father, and her golden boy will not go down alone. From her pocket, she pulls the small lock of hair. She lays it on top of the baby.

"Peace, little soul," she says.

She drops soil onto him, pats the dirt with the shovel, and crouches by the spot to place her hand over it. She is willing the tuber to grow into a beautiful orange dahlia. For a second she believes it will, and that she is still an enchanted girl.

ABOUT THE AUTHOR

Lenore Rowntree grew up in Toronto and now lives in Vancouver. Her writing has appeared in many journals and anthologies including *The Best Canadian Poetry Anthology*. Her play *The Woods at Tender Creek* was produced in Vancouver at the Cultch, and she is a co-editor and contributor to the anthology of life stories *Hidden Lives: coming out on mental illness*. Her novel *Cluck* was a finalist in the 2013 Great BC Novel Contest and will be published in 2016.

ACKNOWLEDGEMENTS

I wish to thank my father for the story of his friends Fran and Dick whose dog died after a walk in High Park and fit perfectly into the toolbox Fran had made in her beginner woodworking class. The carpenter I met in Slabtown so many years ago I have forgotten his name, but who told me about the power of a black fox to bring unexpected people together. My friends Pierre Lebel, Avie Perel-Panar and Eve Chapple for their dovetail inspirations and images. My friend Anita Perel-Panar with whom I have shared so many dinnertime stories I have lost count, although I'm certain many have surfaced in this collection. And finally Katrin Horowitz for her careful and patient editing.